D1529001

The Reindeer Ranch

A Sweet Romance Story

C.H. Eryl

© Cheryl Rush Cowperthwait 2021

ISBN: 9798468198377

Cover: Lilia Lalova

Editor: Jeff Ford

Formatted: KH Formatting

All rights reserved. This book or any portion thereof may not be reproduced or used in any manner without the express written permission of the publisher except for the use of brief quotations in a book review.

Dedication

This book is dedicated to all my lovely readers who asked for more, thank you!

Originally this book was a short story included in a book dedicated to short Christmas stories, full of Christmas themed delights to bring the warm feeling of the season home.

You asked for more of the story.

Here it is in the complete novel.

Please enjoy!

CHAPTER 1

I have my hands full, one hand on Ethan and the other pulling Mattie. The cold, north wind blows my auburn hair over my head and smackdab into my eyes. My mind throbs trying to balance the tilting platter of responsibilities resting on my shoulders. It's only a few weeks before Christmas and I still have so much to do, and now daycare has called for me to pick up my children early. They both have fevers and need to go home. *Just great,* I think, my mind racing on how I can get my work done on time.

"Mommy, I don't feel good," Mattie says with a groan, her hand rubbing her forehead. "I'm hot."

Even though I have a tight grasp on one hand, Mattie works her right hand to unzip the coat, shaking it off her shoulder and down her arm.

"No, Mattie. Not yet. First, let's get into the car, and then you can get out of your jacket." I stop to pull Ethan next to us to rethread the jacket onto Mattie's arm.

A firetruck rounds the curve, horns blaring as it heads toward some unseen emergency.

Ethan runs to the edge of the sidewalk and takes a toddling step—

"Ethan!" I leap up and race to snatch him before he gets any farther.

His face turns to look at me as he slips and stumbles into the street.

The firetruck races on, feet away from my child.

"Did you see it, Mommy? The firetruck? It goes fast and makes pretty colors." His face beams.

Shaking, I raise little Ethan to his feet, dust him off, and hug him to my chest. "Oh, Ethan. You scared me. Yes, I saw the firetruck. Come on, let's get to the car. It's starting to snow."

Big, fluffy snowflakes fall from a grey sky, pelting us. I've parked down the block, because so many cars are parked near the daycare center. It's that time of year for colds and flu, and I imagine many parents are here picking up sick children. After buckling my seven-year-old and four-year-old into their car seats, I slip into the Volvo's driver's seat. Taking a deep breath, I start the engine. It kicks over with a low rumble. Thanking my lucky stars, I pat the dashboard and pull onto the road. The car is old, but dependable and paid off.

After my divorce last year, I moved home. Greg had taken everything we had out from under me. Well, anything of monetary value. I didn't tell my family about our troubles until it was too late. I had sold the bedroom furniture, the living room set, China hutch, and dishes. I kept the children's bedroom furniture and called my parents looking for a place to live. They watched my children as I worked two jobs to save for a place to move, as well as a decent car. The Volvo had been cheap—so cheap, in fact, I continually wondered what was wrong with it. Dad inspected it before I signed the papers and didn't find anything noticeably wrong. Last month, I finally paid it off, free and clear. The thought brings me a hard-earned smile.

I work for our city of Hope Falls, a small community but full of wonderful people. My job is the event organizer. It pays decently and keeps a roof over our heads, allowing us a two-bedroom apartment. I'm still struggling to get new vendors for the Christmas Extravaganza. During the last several days, some vendors cancelled at the last minute. And now I have two sick children to tend to. Rubbing the deep furrows on my forehead, I sigh.

Flipping on the turn signal, I turn and see our apartment complex up the road as I hear a sudden *pop*. The car swerves, but I quickly gain control and limp it into the parking place for our apartment. Shaking my head, I exit the car and kick the flat tire. I take Mattie out of her seat, walk around to Ethan's side, and scoop him from his. I rush to our doorway to get out of the snow, unlocking the door and hurrying them inside.

Rita, my neighbor, sticks her head out the door. "Hon, are you okay?"

"Yeah, I guess so. Both Mattie and Ethan were sent home with a fever, and I just got a flat. It's not the way I planned for today, but what can you do?" I shrug.

"I'm sorry to hear the children are sick. A flat, you said?"

"Yes. I'm just lucky it didn't happen until we were almost home. I don't know what I would have done with my two little ones, sick and all."

"Well, hon, I can't watch your kids, them being sick, and me with my medical issues …"

"No, no. I wouldn't think of asking you to do that. I thought if their fever breaks, maybe my mom could watch them the next few days. And maybe lend me her car. I don't want to buy a new tire right now, not with Christmas around the corner." I peer through my door at my children lying on the couch.

"Hey, I know what. Let me call my brother, Brian. He's pretty good at fixing things. Maybe he could take off that tire and patch it for you."

"Goodness no. Look at the snow falling. It will be up to the bumper in no time."

"Nonsense. You need help. You just go in there and take care of those little ones and let me help with one of your worries. Remember, share your worries and cut them in half!" She disappears behind her closed door before I can reply.

CHAPTER 2

I strip out of my coat and gloves, then grab the thermometer from the bathroom cabinet to check Mattie first. The reading is 100.2, so elevated but not terribly so. Ethan's is 101. I call their pediatrician and am given the same old story; keep them hydrated and give them a children's aspirin.

After settling them down with fluffy pillows and blankets on the couch, I check my watch—two p.m. I can still make some calls to see if I can rally up some other vendors. The good thing about my job is I can do most of it by computer and phone, at least the initial contact. I'd still have to go into the office for the vendors to complete the contracts and collect payments, but I can handle that.

Later on, Mattie comes into the kitchen hungry. I glance at the clock and it's already five-thirty. I peel an apple, cut it into slices, and carry the plate into the living room. It will give them something to nibble on while I open a big can of chicken noodle soup. While it's heating, I prepare a couple of grilled cheese sandwiches, thinking, *When they're sick, these foods usually go down without a fight.*

Hearing a knock at the door, I slide the pan off the burner and ensure the knob is in the off position. Opening the door, I find Rita there wringing her hands.

"Mercy. I've been trying to call you for hours."

"Come in, Rita." I invite her with a wave of my hand through the doorway, but Rita takes one look at the kids on the couch and shakes her head. I slip out the doorway to join Rita. "What's wrong?"

"Nothing is wrong, Darci. I called you when Brian came out. I thought you'd like to meet him, since he was taking off your tire to be fixed."

"Rita, you didn't call him, did you?"

She nods and smiles. "He's already been here, removed the tire and had it fixed and put it right back on for you."

I slump against the wall. It was thoughtful for Rita to call him, but now I wonder how much this will cost. If I spoke to him first, I could have delayed repairing the tire and saved paying someone to fix and replace it.

"Don't go looking all worried. Brian says it should last you for a while. And"—she nudges me— "he got it all for free. The man he took the tire to owed him a favor, so he collected on it and saved you a few bucks."

"Why in the world would he do that, Rita? Look. I didn't want charity …" Heat rises up to my face. The one thing I'm sure about in life is you don't get something for nothing.

Rita frowns. "I-I was just trying to help you out."

I run a hand through my curls and puff a deep breath. "I'm sorry, Rita. That came out all wrong. I guess I'm overly tense with the kids home and trying to line up vendors for the Christmas event. I let my stress get to me and, well, please forgive me?" I give her a puppy dog look.

Rita perks right up and waves a nonchalant hand. "No worries." Her grey eyes shimmer again. "Hey, so *you're* the one who gets all the people for the town's events." She shakes her head, chuckling. "You won't believe this."

"What? What won't I believe?"

"It's Brian. He has all sorts of critters at his ranch. Maybe he could have them in a roundabout pen for the children to look at?"

I scratch my face in thought. "What kind of animals?"

Rita's mouth splits into a half-moon smile. "For one thing, he has reindeer."

Mattie, who had slipped up behind me without my knowing, yells, "Reindeer! Mommy, I want to see the reindeer."

Rita giggles underneath her hand.

"We'll see, Mattie. Now go back inside. I'm almost finished talking with our neighbor. Rita, I'll think about it and call you in a while. I have the children's dinner on the stove, and I need to get them fed, bathed, and to bed." I say waving goodbye before closing the door.

Later, after dinner and bathing the children and myself tucked snuggly into bed, I can finally sit and catch my breath. The thought of reindeer flashes into mind. I already lost a vendor who was to bring his ponies for pony rides. Parents told me the kids love them, but he had retired and sold his animals. A light sparks in my mind. *Yes, I've already booked a Santa. What would be better than having reindeer next to Santa's booth?* The idea seems perfect.

I dial Rita. "Hello, Rita, this is Darci. I hope I'm not calling too late."

We chat for several minutes and I hang up after getting her brother's phone number. It's almost nine o'clock, no time to be making a business call. *I'll call tomorrow and ask him what I owe for him taking care of the tire.*

CHAPTER 3

The morning breaks sunny and clear; the small lawn in front of our apartment glimmers in the sunlight. I smile. Something is magical about fresh snow close to Christmastime, bringing back childhood memories of sledding and ice skating. Checking on Mattie first, I find her temperature has come down but still not normal. Ethan is still sleeping so silently I shut the door and leave him to rest while I brush Mattie's hair, then sit her at the table with a bowl of cereal and juice.

Nibbling on a fingernail, I reach for the phone. Normally, placing a business call is a no-brainer, but this is Rita's brother. He had already come out and fixed my tire, after all. I blow away my pent-up breath. *I don't even know his last name.* I grab the slip of paper and punch in the number and wait as it rings … and rings. As I'm ready to hang up, someone answers in a very deep voice.

"Hello, is this Brian?"

After a pause, he says, "Yes, I'm Brian."

"This is Darci. Rita's next-door neighbor. The one you came and fixed the tire for."

Laughter booms from the other end. "Hi, Darci, Rita's next-door neighbor that I had the tire fixed for."

I stay quiet. Him repeating my words feels odd, but really friendly.

"Hello?" Brian asks in wonder.

"Ah, yes. Hi. I wanted to thank you. I'm sorry I didn't see you or know you had come out and did all that. I was preoccupied with phone calls, and my children were home sick."

"Hey, no sweat at all. How well do you know Rita?"

"Not very well. She usually catches me in a hurry in or out. We haven't spent much time chatting."

I hear him chuckling under his breath. "She can talk an ear off. Look. You don't owe me anything. It didn't cost me anything but a bit of time."

"But it was freezing cold and snowing!"

"It wasn't anything, and I was happy to help. It made my sister feel good knowing you were looked after. I try to keep her happy, so this was just another way to bring Rita a smile."

"You're being awfully considerate. I really do appreciate your help, and again, I want to apologize for not even meeting you while you were here. I could have at least brought you out some hot chocolate."

"Now you're tempting my tummy," he says, laughing.

I like his laugh; he seems very easy-going. "I actually called you for another reason, too. Rita mentioned you have reindeer."

"She did, did she? Yes, as a matter of fact, I do. Does that make me sound crazy?"

"Not in the least. You see, I'm the city's event planner, and it just so happens we have a huge event in a couple of weeks."

"Oh yes, the Christmas Extravaganza. What would this town be like without a big Christmas shindig? I enjoy it most every year."

"Then you know it takes a lot of vendors to maintain interest. I've booked a Santa, and I thought if you aren't scheduled anywhere on Saturday the nineteenth, I would love for you to be a vendor. I could place you close to the Santa booth. I could even wave the vendor fee."

"My reindeer aren't scheduled to be anywhere that day, so yeah, that sounds like a plan. I'd still want to pay the vendor fee, though. The city needs all it can get to continue hosting these wonderful events. It keeps us happy to stay in our own community."

"That is really nice of you. The fees *do* go a long way in helping us prepare for the next events, so thank you for that. I have some forms you'll need to sign. Could you come by the office after the weekend to sign them?"

"So, how is that little boy and girl of yours?"

"Um, better? I think?"

"I was thinking, if they feel better and are up to it, you could bring them out for a sneak peek at the reindeer on Saturday. You could bring the forms, and I'd sign them while you're here. Next week, I'll be away."

"Go there to see the reindeer …"

"Yes, Mommy, yes! Please, can we go see the reindeer?" Mattie asks, overhearing me.

Another round of laughter meets my ears. "I guess you heard my daughter. Can I let you know tomorrow evening? Her temperature is down a bit this morning, but I don't want her to be contagious."

"No, sure, that's fine. I thought they might get a kick out of it, and we could take care of the business end of things at the same time."

"Trust me. I think your offer will be a magical cure-all once Ethan hears of this opportunity, but I'll call you tomorrow evening to let you know for certain and arrange a time to meet."

"Call anytime. I'll be around."

"It was very nice meeting you by phone, Brian. Thank you again for fixing my tire. I really do feel bad for not at least going out there to meet you."

"Don't be. It's all good. Like I said, it made Rita happy, and that's good enough for me."

"Okay then. I guess I'll speak to you tomorrow, um, to let you know about Saturday. Goodbye."

"Bye, Darci."

I hang up the phone and realize I feel flushed. Flushed! By a phone call. I shake my head and go to check on Ethan. When I take his temperature, it *is* down, but not as much as Mattie's.

"Are you hungry this morning?"

"Yes, enough to eat a bear, Mommy."

"A bear?" I ask, chuckling.

"Yeah, I don't want to eat a horse. I like horses."

I laugh and tousle his hair. "Come on to the kitchen. I'll get you some cereal."

"Aww, I was hoping for pancakes." His lower lip turns down in a frown I can't ignore.

"Okay, little man. Pancakes it is."

"Yes! I'm going to tell sissy," he says, running off and calling Mattie's name non-stop.

I pour a cup of coffee, then stare at my phone lying on the kitchen counter and smile.

After breakfast, it's time to clean up the kids and get them situated so I can call the other vendors and make contact at work. I also need to call daycare to tell them not to expect Mattie and Ethan until at least Monday. The day whirls by with a clutter of things getting taken care of, one by one.

Exhausted by eight p.m., I crawl into bed with a book I've been meaning to read, but it falls from my hands shortly after I open it.

The next morning, the kids are wide awake and jumping on my bed before sunrise. I wrestle them into the covers and feel their heads. By touch, they don't feel feverish, and by actions they are all better, which makes me very happy. I cuddle them until their wildness gives way to rhythmic breathing and leave them to sleep in my bed as I shower and get ready for the day.

Mom bustles in with a sack full of books to read to her grandchildren so I can run to the office to take care of a few things and pick up a contact for the festival, as well as a receipt book for Saturday. It's difficult for me to keep my mind on business, as it keeps drifting to the stranger's voice on the phone.

Stop that! He's either married or some kind of convict. I put him out of my mind. Mostly.

CHAPTER 4

Meanwhile, Brian finds himself in rising turmoil. He has offered to do something kind for his sister's neighbor—a woman raising two children by herself after her divorce. But something has tugged at him when speaking with her, something he thought he had buried after his last love had left him empty. Swearing not to ever put himself in a similar position, he finds himself all too close to the fire.

Samantha had been in his life for five years—her and her son, Billy. She had been a light in his life, and Billy? Billy had brought out the best in him—the feelings of what it meant to be a father. Billy's father was out of the picture, a conman doing time, and Brian found himself eager to fill that role for Billy as his romance with Samantha grew.

That was what led him away from his company—an internet company he'd taken from startup to the big time. When he sold it and bought a ranch, he filled it with the animals that brought Billy smiles and laughter. In the end, it was a veritable petting zoo with ponies, goats, sheep, horses, cows, and his last acquisition, the reindeer. Shortly after buying the ranch, Samantha felt the need to spread her wings. It turned out the quiet life on a ranch wasn't to her liking. She collected most of their things and left one day when he had taken the animals to a children's party. They left him by leaving behind a goodbye note, his broken heart, and their personal items she didn't have time to pack. He'd fallen in love with both Samantha and Billy, and they were gone. He vowed to never let his heart be stomped on like that again.

He wonders if it's simply his loneliness drawing him to the voice on the phone. *Sure, Rita said repeatedly that her neighbor was a looker, but she's always trying to fix me up with someone or another. And frankly, I'm not after a looker. I want someone who I can relate to, who enjoys the simple things in life ... No, this is a business arrangement.* He vows to keep it that way.

After putting in a few hours at the office, I return home through the slush-ridden roads in time for Mom to drive home before dark settles in. Usually, I'd be annoyed when Mattie and Ethan brought their armloads of toys into the living room, but now I can only smile and be thankful their fevers had broken and they're up to their normal vigor.

I hug them next to me and plop onto the couch in the midst of tickles and giggles. Enjoying our time together, I make a big bowl of popcorn and we watch Disney movies until they fall asleep on the couch. I carry them to bed and change them into pajamas before tucking them in.

It suddenly hits me that I didn't called Brian to give him the update on the children and whether I can meet him at his ranch tomorrow. I check the clock—only 8 p.m. Grabbing the phone, I shuffle papers to find where I put his number. I smirk. *It won't be a bad idea to add it to my contact list—after all, he would be a vendor. I might have to contact him in the future.* My eyebrows wiggle at the thought.

"Hello." His deep timbre sounds so close to my ear, as if he's in the same room instead of miles away. I hear someone in the background laughing.

"I'm sorry to be calling at this hour. This is Darci. I wanted to let you know my children are feeling their normal little selves and would enjoy the outing to your ranch tomorrow if the offer is still open."

"Darci, um, sure. That sounds fine. What time do you think you'll be coming by?"

"I was thinking after lunchtime. Say, around one o'clock?"

"I better let you know how to get there."

"Okay, just a moment please. I need to grab some paper." The doorbell rings. "Oh shoot, hang on, someone's at the door. I'll be right back."

He chuckles on the other end.

I open the door. "Yes?"

In front of my door stands a dark and ruggedly handsome man with a phone to his ear. He breaks out with a grin from ear to ear. "Darci?"

I hear the voice echo through my phone. "Oh! Brian? What are you doing here?" My words tumble over my tongue. I feel positive my tongue is hanging out of my mouth. I disconnect the call, realizing how silly I must look.

"I couldn't resist. I was next door at my sister's house, feasting on pizza. I thought, if you don't mind, I would stop by and draw you a little map. It's not hard to find once you know how to get there."

Rita pokes her head out of her door and waves.

"Sure. No. I mean yes, that would be fine. Gaw, excuse the mess in the living room. The kids usually pick up after themselves, but today is the first day they've felt better. I didn't want to ruin it by sticking to the rules."

He nods. "Would you feel better if Rita came in with me? I know we just met."

I wave my hand dismissively. "It's fine. She knows you're here, so I'll have a witness." I wink, catching him off-guard. *Gaw, what did it sound like I thought he was? A serial killer?* My face grows red roses on my cheeks.

"Listen. We have almost a half pizza left and some beer. Would you like some?" He rubs his hands together subconsciously.

This man intrigues me. My mind whirls. With his sister next door, I don't need to be nervous with him in the apartment, and a pizza would allow us more time to get to know each other. "Pizza. How could I refuse? Tell me it's pepperoni."

He looks dead serious. "What? Is there another kind?" He waves and points to Rita's door with one finger to his lips, slinking toward her door.

I shake my head. He is already crawling under my skin. I mean, I had just met him, but he is so unpretentious and seems fun.

With a huff and puff, he hurries to my door with a pizza box and two beers in hand. I like that. He doesn't bring a whole six pack, inferring we would drink the night away. He slides the box onto the table before cracking a beer and offering one to me with a raised brow. "I should have asked. Do you like beer or even drink?"

"Yes to both. I rarely have the opportunity. When I'm not at work, I'm home with the children, and by the time they go to bed …" I shrug with my arms out, palms facing the ceiling.

"Understandable. So tonight is a golden opportunity. Cheers to you, Darci." We both take a swig and tear into a piece of pizza. "If you follow the road here"—he points to his drawing— "and turn left on the gravel road, it will lead you down a meandering road. At the point when you first start double guessing yourself, you should see the cabin. Head to the cabin, then we'll switch to my rig, and I'll take you and your children out to see the reindeer." He takes another slow gulp of beer, lifting his eyes to see if I have questions.

I'm not looking at the map; I'm looking at his oatmeal-colored, cable weave sweater. His sleeves are pushed up, showing strong forearms. I've always had a thing for strong arms. My eyes wander to his chiseled jawline. I avert my eyes from staring at his face when I discover he is looking up. My eyes fall to the hand-drawn map on the napkin. "Great, I think I can find it easy enough."

"Call me if you have any trouble finding the road." He polishes off the slice of pizza and washes it down with another swallow of his beer. "Okay, I'll leave you the rest of the pizza and head home. By the way, is your tire holding up after the patch was done?"

"Yes. As a matter of fact, I had to get out for a bit today, and it didn't give me any problems." My mind flits to the papers lying on the counter. I could just as easily have him sign them while he's here.

He pushes back the chair and saunters to the door. "If there isn't anything else, I'll see you tomorrow. It's nice meeting you, Darci."

"And you, Brian. See you tomorrow." I shut the door and lean against it. I turn the lock and float in a daze into the kitchen with the image of his face still locked in my mind's eye. His almost black, wavy hair hung over the back of his sweater, and his five o'clock shadow seemed to fit his rugged look. His green eyes were a blend of emeralds spread across dew-kissed grass, and his lips looked like they have a habit of smiling. I grin, thinking I've never had a flat tire bring such good luck, and tomorrow we will see his ranch and the reindeer.

CHAPTER 5

Saturday comes with gentle rays of sunshine lighting up the day's possibilities. I wake early and take a nice, long shower with conflicting thoughts of the outing scheduled for later today. Part of me is excited for the possibility of connecting with Brian again, but a deeper part is worried. I finally have stabilized my life and the life of my children. These feelings toward Brian don't fit into my plan. I scrub the soapy lather in my hair as if I can wash away his image and his voice. Completing my shower, I step out to towel dry. Wrapping myself in it, I head to the closet and select jeans, a long-sleeved plaid shirt and the red sweater I love.

The aroma of fried bacon, hash browns, and scrambled eggs wafts through the apartment, stirring Mattie and Ethan from their beds. The quiet of the morning shatters with the noise of the children and their morning antics. My eyes gloss over in thought. I have to think about them, and I can't very well let another man into their lives only to turn them upside down when he gets tired of us and leaves. My lips form a tight line. *No. One quick trip to see the reindeer and nothing more.* Feeling better about my decision, I dish up breakfast, pour coffee, and then gather the scattered toys from yesterday. I hold off telling the children they get to see the reindeer until after their baths and changing their clothes for the day.

While Mattie and Ethan romp in the living room, cartoons blare in the background loud enough to drown out the sound of the vacuum cleaner and my lingering thoughts. By the time I finish with the morning chores, I've reduced the thoughts of Brian to mere dust bunnies hiding under the bed. Soon, I'd Swiffer away those too.

Lunch comes and goes. I interrupt Mattie's and Ethan's fussing over the card game's rules and sit them down, saying, "I thought if you both felt up to it, we'd go for a drive."

"Where to, Mommy?" Ethan asks.

"We've been invited to see reindeer."

"Reindeer! Reindeer!" Mattie shrieks, hopping up and down in the living room.

"Yes, reindeer. The nice man who fixed my tire the other day, as it turns out, has reindeer and will be one of the people at the Christmas Extravaganza. While we are visiting, I'll have him sign some papers that will allow him to bring them."

"Are these Santa's reindeer?" Mattie asks, eyes wide in wonder.

"No, sweetie, but they will probably be close to Santa's booth at the event." I smile as I see the excitement in their eyes.

Mattie nods and whispers to her brother, "They could be Santa's extras. Like the ones in training."

"Go grab your coats, hats, and mittens. We don't want to keep the reindeer waiting."

In a zoom, they race to their closets and hurry back, a blur of colors dancing around my feet. I laugh as I get them ready for the trip.

"I wish we could have a reindeer, Mommy," Mattie gushes as I fasten her into the car seat.

"We don't have space for a reindeer. They need special care and a nice big place to roam."

"If we move to a nice big place, then we could get one?" Mattie asks.

I can only smile and shake my head at her. *Goodness knows she would have a whole farm of animals if she could.*

Before heading toward the road to Brian's ranch, I review the napkin-map sitting in the passenger seat next to my phone in case I get lost.

Mattie starts singing "Jingle Bells" with such enthusiasm Ethan and I join in, singing our hearts out. We turn left on the indicated gravel road in no time at all.

"Mommy, does the nice man with reindeer live way out here?" Ethan pushes his hands against his seat to look out the window better.

"That's what he said. He said we follow this road until we think we're lost, and then we'd see his cabin."

"Well," Mattie says smartly, "we should see it soon then, because we've been on this road forever."

Suddenly, around the next curve, the *cabin* comes into view. My jaw drops. It is more like a mansion, with its tall stone and log beams standing high upon a hill. In front of it was the sheen of a frozen pond. I never imagined *this* image when Brian said he lives in a cabin. Its covered porch wraps around the front and down the one side I can see.

"Look, Mommy. See that big place on the hill? Does the man live there?" Mattie asks in awe.

"I guess so, Mattie. We'll stop there to check. I may have made a wrong turn."

We pull into the long driveway in front of the house and hear the bang of the screen door swinging shut. Brian stands on the porch with a cup of something warm in his hand, waving with the other. "I see you found the place. Any troubles?"

"None beside thinking we were lost."

He laughs heartily. "Good thing you kept going. I'd hate for you to miss the reindeer."

"Reindeer, reindeer!" Mattie and Ethan yell.

"Who do we have here?" Brian sits his coffee mug on the table between the rocking chairs and bends down.

"I'm Mattie. This is my little brother Ethan."

"Nice to meet you both. I'm Brian Walters." He proffers his hand, and Ethan gives it a fast jerk up and down while Mattie twists from side to side, smiling.

Mattie eyes the house behind him. "Do you live in this big house all by yourself, or do your parents live here?"

Laughing, Brian stands up. "All by myself. My parents live in another town, but they have a room for when they visit. Okay, everyone, ready to see the reindeer?"

Yeses ring as loud as fireworks.

"Follow me. It's just a short ride, but I have the wagon set up to take you there."

"A wagon?" Mattie stops walking, puzzled.

"Yes, the best kind. The back is filled with hay and has benches and running boards so you can sit up high or down in the hay." Brian winks at Mattie as he leads them around the side of the towering house to where he's connected the small wagon to the back of his tractor. "I have a bigger wagon I use when I get a class full of youngsters out here to ride. That one I hitch to the horses, like I'll do next week."

"Whatcha doing next week?" Ethan asks as I lift him into the wagon.

"Next Friday night, we're riding around the ranch, singing Christmas carols. Then, when we finish, we'll sit by the big bonfire and roast marshmallows, hot dogs, and have hot cocoa."

"I want to come. Can I, Mommy?" Ethan pleads.

I blush. "Ethan, that's not nice to self-invite. This is a private party."

"I'm sorry, Darci. It's my fault I said it that way, thinking you and the kids would enjoy it. It's not what I call a private party. Mostly, it's my sister, who you've met, and some of her longtime friends and their kids. This is sort of a tradition. Once I purchased the ranch, we started doing this to remind us of our childhood. Man, we loved going on hayrides."

"It does sound like a lot of fun. I haven't been on a hayride since I was a teenager. Thank you for thinking of us. Yes, we'd love to come. The kids will enjoy it."

"Yay! I can't wait." Mattie's eyes gleam their excitement.

"It's a plan then. Okay, everyone hold on to the sideboards. It's a bit bumpy until we get going." He walks in front of them and climbs onto a tractor with huge rear tires. He turns and gives me a wink. "Here we go."

We lunge forward as the tractor moves, igniting a roll of laughter.

CHAPTER 6

The crisp air brightens the blush on Darci's cheeks. Brian didn't let it go unnoticed. He's irritated with himself for lining up another event with Darci and her kids. He's falling into the same trap as he has before. Only just meeting Mattie and Ethan, he's fond of them already, and Darci—she takes his breath away. She has an easy way about her, an honesty he feels down to his toes. His sister has briefed him on all that she knows about Darci, and he finds her to be both brave and courageous.

Unlike my previous relationship ... Although he had loved Samantha, it was only after she had left him he discovered she had not only stole his heart, but had made herself comfortable racking up a tidy sum on his credit cards. Frankly, he was amazed he got off as cheap as he did. He gives a mental shrug. Money never has been something important to him, even when he sold his business for more than a person could dream. He likes to keep it as secret as possible; even Rita doesn't know he's a multi-millionaire. He chuckles under his breath, remembering how he let her know he bought the whole ranch for next to nothing because it was a distressed sale. Money has a way of changing most people, and he didn't want to be one of them.

Laughing and having a great time, I play with Mattie and Ethan as we follow a winding road behind the tractor. I haven't had a day this carefree in … I can't remember how long. The road disappears from my vision and is replaced with the view of a red barn. I feel the smile creep across my face. *Like a Santa's workshop.*

The tractor stops. Brian leaps from the seat and hurries to the back of the wagon to remove the safety boards from the end. He offers his hand to me to help me down.

As our hands touch, we both jerk them away for a second, then look at each other.

I laugh, embarrassed. "I'm sorry about that. I think our hands built up static electricity."

Brian just smiles as he helps me get my feet on the ground, then he reaches to help Mattie as I catch Ethan under his arms and lift him out of the wagon.

I whirl around with both children fastened in my hands. "Where are these wonderful reindeer you've said to have?"

"Right through here." He walks beside Mattie, bending over to share some facts about the reindeer.

I can't hear what he's saying, but Mattie's face shows awe.

"I see them, Ethan. Hurry."

Ethan drags me, hurrying to get to where Mattie stands. There in front of them in a wide-open stall are six reindeer with coats of a creamy white changing to a darker brown on their legs and rump. Half of the reindeer have antlers and the other half don't, but they are bigger than the ones with antlers.

"Why do some of the reindeer have antlers?" Mattie asks.

"Well, this is a secret not a lot of people know. Did you know all of Santa's reindeer were girls?"

Mattie gasps. "No. Even Rudolph?" she asks in wonder.

Brian nods. "That's what I think. Do you know why I think that?"

Mattie slowly shakes her head.

"Because, in winter, only the females keep their antlers. So, all those pictures of Santa's reindeer have to be females."

"Wow," Mattie says in surprise.

"I didn't know that," I say, wondering if he made it all up.

"Truth." He leans close to me and whispers, "When you have reindeer, you have to learn all sorts of facts to keep things interesting." He adds a wink.

There he goes again, winking. I wonder if he knows how that simple gesture sends butterflies through my blood veins. "Why do the females keep them, but the males don't?"

"Well, if you look at their size difference, it helps keep things in balance. If they were in the wild and searching for food, the males could knock the females out of the way and eat all the food. Now the females can protect their food source from being bullied from the males. See, she usually will have a calf with her, and they share the same food. By keeping her antlers throughout winter, she can provide food for her little one."

"Can I pet them?" Ethan's hand itches to reach over the perimeter fencing.

"Sure, Ethan. They're very tame and love attention. Do you know what their favorite treats are?"

"Carrots!" Mattie shouts, jumping up and down. "We leave them outside at Christmas so they have something to eat while Santa comes inside."

"You're absolutely correct. They also like apples and even a well-tossed salad. No dressing required," he replies with a grin. "I just so happen to have a bunch of carrots in this bucket. Why don't you each grab one and hold it out to the reindeer."

He doesn't have to ask twice, as the kids plunge their hands into the bucket and hold them near the fence. A beauty of a girl swivels her head, blue eyes catching sight of Mattie's carrot as she approaches. She sticks out her tongue and wraps it around the carrot before delicately chewing it, Mattie petting her side the whole time. Ethan waits his turn until another reindeer catches the carrot's scent and comes to him. The kids are beaming, as even I am. We feed the reindeer until they all have a chance to have a treat, then Brian leads them to another barn.

"I thought while you were here you might like to see the ponies and miniature horses."

"Wow, Mommy. Did you hear that?"

"Yes, Mattie." I meet Brian's gaze. "You have no idea what you've let yourself into. They both love animals, but Mattie doesn't know a critter she couldn't love."

"Ahh, a girl after my own heart." He drops his head with his fist to his heart. "I've loved animals all my life, and I've had more than my share of rescued rabbits, birds, and turtles. I later turned my sights to cows and horses, then, as you see here, everything else."

"So, you're a rancher then?" I ask.

"Hardly! I'm more of a hobbyist. But"—he waves his arm in front of us—"as you can see with the barns, I got a little carried away." He flashes a lopsided grin and shrugs. "That is what I'll be doing next week. I've met with several places that need tamed animals for their causes. Some of them do what I do and bring them to parties for the kids to enjoy, but most of them have places for therapy for Down's children, for handicapped children, and even for those suffering from PTSD. Animals connect with everyone, and since I have more than enough, I'm donating the extras for others to enjoy."

I know I must be staring with my mouth wide open. I can't believe the sort of man who stands in front of me, one who is so caring, giving, and thoughtful of others. The shrill scream of Mattie shakes me from my stupor as I turn to see Mattie skipping to the low gates where a line of heads lean over them.

"Look at them all! Mommy, aren't they beautiful?"

As I glance down the center of the barn, I see no less than twenty miniature horses in every blend of coloring, standing and waiting for the tender hands of a child to pet them. I can't wait to meet every one of them.

"Mr. Brian, could we ride some of the horses?" Mattie asks, her chocolate-brown eyes searching his face.

"If it's okay with your mom, it's okay with me."

Mattie turns her eyes to me, hopeful.

"Do you have some super tame ponies?" I ask, biting my lower lip. "They haven't been on horseback before."

"Yes, all of them are, but we'll saddle up a few of them I'll be placing in new homes on Monday, to keep them ready. I'll take you to the ponies. Follow me, gang."

With whoops and hollers, Mattie and Ethan flank Brian.

He laughs a deep chuckle, and I stand behind them shaking my head. How can Brian be so cooperative to all the children's wants? He didn't even look bothered.

He takes them to the gates with the ponies. "This one is Bella. I thought the name suited her, with her beautiful blue eyes and white coat. The one next to her I call the Dark Knight, since he has a shiny black coat. They are quite the pair, and all the kids love them when I take them on visits."

Mattie's lower lip puckers and pushes down in a near-cry pout, and her eyes glisten.

Brian looks down at her. "Mattie? What's wrong?"

She sniffles and rubs her mittened hand across her nose. "I can't see how you could give them away. They're … They're so wonderful and-and I would want to see them every day."

Brian drops his head and lays a hand over his heart, as if her words had punched a hole into it. "Cheer up, Mattie. You'll make Bella sad. Come on, let's get her saddle, and you can ride her."

She nods, petting Bella's beautiful coat.

Once Brian has saddled both ponies, he leads Mattie into the round, gated area atop Bella while I take Ethan out on Dark Knight. We escort them around and around the arena for what seems like hours, the kids having a wonderful time. I even stop them several times to take pictures of Mattie and Ethan on the ponies. I plan to hang those pictures on their bedroom wall.

After the ponies are in their stalls, Brian announces, "Now it's time to ride to the house, and I'll get our drinks and snacks ready. Who's hungry?"

Cheers erupt around him as we leave the barn and meander to the wagon.

I'm still mystified as to how he had learned to work around children so well; it was like he was a pro in knowing how to get them to change directions without a fuss. Then I nod to myself. *It's what he spent his time doing, by taking the animals to children's parties.* Surely, he can't make enough doing that to pay for this big place and donate his stock to other ranches. He is a mystery. And I love a good mystery.

At the cabin, Brian walks them to the side porch and slips inside.

I settle the kids into the chairs around an oval table.

He comes through the door with two mugs of hot cocoa topped with marshmallows. He dodges inside and brings out two mugs of coffee. "I'll be right back. I picked up a box of doughnuts this morning. I bet there is something for everyone in there."

He opens the box and Mattie and Ethan pick their choices, and I take my all-time favorite—the jelly-filled doughnut—before Brian sits to pass out napkins.

"I feel like I've been on a holiday," I said, relaxing back into the chair.

"This was so fun," Mattie mumbles between bites of doughnut and swigs of cocoa.

"Yeah, I want to do this a bunch of times," Ethan says with powdered sugar on his lips.

"Before I forget, because all of the fun we're having, I brought the papers for you to review and sign for the Christmas event."

"I almost forgot. It's a good thing you remembered. Sure, bring them out."

I retrieve the papers from my purse and slide them in front of Brian.

He turns to the last page and signs the document.

My brows furrow. "Aren't you going to read it?"

"Has it changed over the last few years?" He raises a brow.

"I don't think so, but this is my first year doing the event."

"I'm sure it's the same as it has always been. Things don't change very often in Hope Falls," he winks. "What is the fee for my reindeer? And yes, before you ask, I'll be bringing my own enclosure. It allows the children to see through the open metal panels. They hook together and are low enough for them to feed treats and pet them."

"This isn't your first rodeo, right?"

"Right." He gives a knowing look.

"The fee is fifty dollars, but I really hate to charge you, after all you've done for us."

"No worries. Like I said, I'm glad to support our town and the event. It makes it good for all of us."

"If you don't mind me asking, what do you do? I mean, as far as your regular job."

"Oh, this is my regular job … now. I had a small business years ago that I sold, and, well, I did okay, so now I enjoy this sort of thing."

My eyes widen as my brows lift into my bangs. I scratch my head. I can't imagine what business he could have had to support him, the ranch, and the payments on the big house. Maybe it is family land?

"Thank Mr. Walters for all the fun today, kids. It will be dark soon, and we need to get home."

My ears fill with the deflated sighs and, "Aww, do we have to?"

"Thank you, Mr. Walters," Mattie and Ethan echo.

"You made me sound like my parents. I prefer to be called Brian, if it's all the same to you."

"Okay, Brian it is!" Mattie chimes back, smiling.

I lead them to the Volvo and secure them into their seats.

Brian meets me at the car, hands behind his back, smiling.

I look at him, puzzled.

"Did you forget something?" He brings the papers from behind his back with a fifty-dollar bill on top.

"Oh! Silly me, and I haven't given you a receipt yet." I dig through my purse for the receipt book until he lays his hand on my arm. The warmth of it spreads all over me.

"It's okay. You can give it to my sister when you get home. It's almost dark, and I'd rather you get home safe and sound than to worry about a receipt. Remember, you're traveling on a repaired tire." The look in his eyes are softened but hold a pinch of concern on the edges.

"If you're sure that's all right, I'll leave it with Rita once I get the children settled."

"Thank you. I'd hate to sit here worried whether you made it safely home. Now, with you giving Rita the receipt, I'll know you did."

"How will that let you know?"

He chortles. "Don't worry. She'll call me before you even reach your apartment."

I laugh and nod as I climb into the car. Turning to wave goodbye, I almost smack him in the face; he had leaned down to my window.

"I just wanted to thank you for coming out with the kids. It's been a great afternoon."

My cheeks flush to a hot pink. "It's us who should thank you over and over again. We had the best time. Thank you, Brian."

"Now, don't forget. Christmas carols and hayrides next Friday night." He stands upright, waving goodbye before folding his arms.

I give him a thumbs-up and turn around to take the path to the main road. My eyes dart back to see the house illuminated my rearview mirror. *We'll get to come back in only a week. I think it'll be a very long week until next Friday.*

I write out the receipt as soon as I get home and go to Rita's apartment. For once, Rita doesn't want to stay and chat. She looks a little off, but I have to rush back to my apartment since Mattie is calling out.

Chapter 7

In no time, Rita reaches for her phone to call her brother.

"Hi, sis. I told Darci if she brought you the receipt then I'd know they all got home safe and sound."

A pause stretches on the other end.

"Sis? What's wrong?"

"I don't know how to say it, so I'll just say it. Samantha called. Her and Billy are back. She, well, she called me and hinted that they would be moving back to the ranch."

It's Brian's time to be silent. He stops pacing as he usually does while talking on the phone and plunges into the couch, one hand rubbing his forehead.

"Brian? Are you still there?"

"Yeah, sis, still here. What rotten timing. You know I'll be out of town most of next week with the delivery of the animals. What did she tell you?"

Rita sighs. "You know her. She talked and talked a mile a minute, but it was like a bird flapping its wings. I had to sit down and decipher most of it. What I got out of it all was she's tired of the change of scenery and she had always been a small-town girl. Can you believe that? Anyway, she landed at her family's place but said she couldn't wait to get back to the ranch and the peace and quiet."

"You know as well as I do I can't have her and Billy back in my life. It's taken me years to get over her leaving and jerking

Billy out from underneath me. I don't trust her, and I don't trust that con of a man she had married before. I'm sorry for Billy's sake, but I won't roll out the carpet for her return."

"I'm glad to hear it, Brian. I was worried you'd take her back. She turned you into a different person back then. You were someone she was happy just to get whatever she could from you. I know you loved her, loved her son like your own, but she'll hurt you, Brian. She'll hurt you beyond recovery, I fear."

"No need to worry. I'll take care of it. I'll have a company come out tomorrow to install a gate to block the drive to the house. That way I don't have to worry about them sitting on my porch when I get back. If she calls again and tries to get you to open the gate, just let her know you don't have the code. And, Rita, don't mention Darci. I don't want Samantha thinking something is going on and then hassle Darci and her kids."

Rita coughs. "Well, is something going on?"

"They were here today for me to sign those papers for the Christmas event. I had a good time showing Mattie and Ethan the reindeer and ponies. It was the best afternoon I've had in a while, to be honest. They'll join us for the Friday night caroling hayride, but, other than that, we are just having a good time in each other's company."

"Um-hum," Rita says, her voice lilting.

"Honest, that's all there is to it. I'm not looking to get into the same mess I came out of, and now with Samantha back in town, well, I don't want to give her any reason to bother Darci. She could wreck a good friendship. Darci is so easy to be around, and I never have to second guess what she is thinking or, well, any of the stuff I always worried about with Samantha. I would rather deal with Samantha and ensure she knows there isn't a life for her at the ranch. I wish I could postpone this trip, but people are counting on me."

"Don't worry, Brian. Maybe she'll get tired of waiting for you to return and leave. Anyway, if you have the gate installed, that'll keep her away at least until you come home. Do you know when that'll be?"

"Most likely Friday morning after I make the last delivery."

"Good, then I can come out early and help you prep for our special Friday hayride."

"That will be great, sis. I look forward to this every year. Call me if you need me. I'll call you back if I'm with someone when you call, okay?"

"You're a good brother and good man, Brian Walters. Love you."

"Love you too, sis. Goodnight."

He hangs up, still dazed by hearing Samantha has returned to town. He even surprises himself for not being happy to hear Samantha was back; after all, that was all he wanted after she left. Back then, he had wanted her to come back no matter the cost. Now worries creep inside. What game is she playing? Dragging Billy into it makes him even angrier. Part of him wants to call her to tell her to leave him alone, but the other part feels like he should keep quiet and ensure he has a security gate installed tomorrow before he even thinks of talking to her again. Just hearing about her has doused cold water over him, breaking the perfect afternoon he had enjoyed, but he has to be thankful he didn't know she was back in town earlier. At least he had a great afternoon without her spoiling it. Until now.

Clicking off the outside lights, he locks all the doors and retreats to the warmth of the den to get lost in his music before heading to bed. Tomorrow he can fix things and feel a lot better. Brian calls his longtime friend and associate from the old days and, with Luke's help, secures a gate installation by noon, then falls exhausted to bed.

By daybreak, he and a few locals are busy adding a fence line across the front of the property to further secure the way to his house. In over five years, he never felt the need to do any of these things, but now…

It's already been a long day by the time he hitches his live-stock trailer to his truck and prepares it for the trip. In the morning he will only have to load the ponies, a few saddle horses, and the baby goats and lambs. He has looked forward to a leisurely trip and visit at the four stops, but now wishes he had done this last week so he could be home to ensure nothing awful happens. He has to put his trust in the security gate to keep Samantha away. She has an unnerving self-entitlement attitude he previously thought was just her way of compensating about her lackluster ex and her being a new divorcee. Time has cleared his vision. Hindsight has a way of giving twenty-twenty vision and then some.

CHAPTER 8

Back at the cabin, he throws a steak on the grill and turns the packet of potatoes. He hates burnt potatoes. He slips inside to uncork a bottle of wine and finish the salad. It's moments like these when he really misses not having someone special with him, someone to share the day with, someone to watch the sunset. When he thinks of that someone, the picture that comes into his mind is Darci. He shrugs and sighs. He hardly knows anything about her except the easy feeling he has being around her and how the world seems a little bit brighter when she's near.

Sipping on his glass of wine, he checks the steak. "Perfection," he says aloud as he plates it and the foil-covered potatoes, taking them inside to eat. He sits and flips on the television to catch the weather. As he takes his first bite of steak, his cellphone rings.

He doesn't recognize the number and almost answers, thinking it might be Darci, but, by the second ring, the ringtone stops. He's suspicious and scrolls through the recent numbers and locates the ones from Darci, and this is a different number. He shivers. It must be Samantha on a new phone he doesn't have in his contact list. The thought makes his drink taste sour. He moves around the rest of the meal on his plate, mostly. His appetite disappeared with the timing of the phone call.

Early Monday morning, he feeds the rest of the animals and prepares for his part-time help to care for them while he's gone with strict instructions to not open the gate to anyone. Once he has loaded the animals, he double checks the house, arms the alarm, and jumps into his truck, ready to get a move on and return home to take care of the loose ends he feels trying to cling to his neck.

Fortune shines on him as he makes his stops on Monday—no storms to contend with and, being so close to the holidays, the ranches are pretty bare of the usual visitors, making it easier to chat with the new owners and visit a bit before heading to the next ones.

By the time Thursday morning rolls around, Brian feels like his old self. Everything has gone well, with no more mysterious phone calls or anyone from home calling with bad news. He makes his last drop off Thursday late afternoon and hugs the last two ponies goodbye. It makes him both happy and sad, as these two had been the first two ponies he'd bought, and they were the ones to light up Billy's eyes and bring Samantha a smile. It's hard letting them go, but it's for the best. As he gets back in his truck, it all feels right, and he isn't too far away that he can't stop by from time to time to visit.

Checking his watch, he knows he has time to get to the ranch, but it will put him there in the early morning hours, and, since they're having the hayride that day, he decides to drive halfway and rest overnight. There will be plenty to make ready once he gets home.

Friday morning greets him with blue skies and paper-thin white clouds stretching so thin, dots of blue show through. It is good to see his travels won't include a major snowstorm; all he wants to do is make it home and prepare for the evening event.

He pulls up to his new gate at 1:30 p.m., enters his code, and waits for the gate to roll away. After he pulls the livestock trailer through, he hits the key fob to close the gate. He idles as he waits for the gate to close and lock into place. A smile reflects in his rearview mirror. Punching the gas pedal, he hurries along his road, smiling as his cabin comes into view and a bigger smile yet when he sees Rita is already there.

Buzzing past his house, he turns to drop off his trailer by the barns. He checks on the animals to ensure his help had fed them. He's a fortunate man to have help he can rely on when he's traveling. He heads for home and the constant chatter of his sister.

Rita rushes to the door as he enters, ready to be scooped up in a hug.

He laughs.

She has her hands dusty in cake batter by the looks of it, already chirping up a storm. She tells him the RSVPs had all come in, and the hayride should be packed with the friends and kids of theirs from the past years. Rita has made enough cupcakes to fill a school cafeteria and is chirping away about how many hot dogs, buns, and chips they have. The stove holds a big pot of simmering chili to keep everyone warm, not to mention copious amounts of hot chocolate. Stacks of blankets lay on the couch for keeping warm on the ride.

Brian sneaks a cupcake off the latest platter and is rewarded by a punch to his arm for it, but she laughs and waves him out of the kitchen.

Suddenly, he feels energized. Rita only really comes out during holidays, and she has the run of the kitchen and stands over it like a little red hen. It gives his spirits a lift. She has a heart condition and takes life slow and easy—unless it's any holiday, then she pours her heart and soul into it as she's doing for this hayride.

Brian leaves to the barns and prepares the big wagon for the festivities. He opens and spreads lots of hay into the back so it will make a nice, deep nest for everyone to wallow into. This wagon has side benches and a big, open middle where most of the kids like to ride. He has a cover he can use in case of snow, but the weather is wonderful; he couldn't have hoped for better. It's forecasted to be clear but chilly tonight. Once the wagon is ready, he adds the large bells on each corner with big red bows. Standing back, he grins.

CHAPTER 9

His phone rings; his stomach drops. He looks at the number and hesitantly answers, “Hello?”

“Hi, Brian. This is Darci.”

His spirits lift with the sound of her voice.

“I forgot to ask what time we should come out for the hayride. I went to Rita’s apartment, but no one answered.”

“Good to hear from you, Darci. Sorry about that. The last time you were here, time got away from us somehow. Oh, well, Rita is already here and baking up a storm in the kitchen. She really enjoys the chance to get out and do fun things. We plan the hayride at around seven o’clock. And then we’ll have the bonfire and all the good eats.”

“I wish I would have known Rita was cooking, I could have helped her.”

A big smile washes across his face. “She would have enjoyed your company, but she can be a hen in the henhouse. She has her ways of doing things and knows exactly what she wants to do.”

She laughs. “I bet she does. Well, if you don’t mind, we would like to get there a little early. The kids are a bit anxious to arrive, if you know what I mean. They’ve been hounding me for hours.”

“Come anytime! Really, I mean it. This is supposed to be a festive day. I’d hate to see them come for just a few hours when they are welcome any time you want to come by.” Brian bangs a fist against his head. He just can't stop himself when talking to her. "Oh, I forgot to tell you, since I've been away all week, I had an entry gate installed, and I'll let you know the keycode."

"Uhm … you probably shouldn't be giving out your security gate code," she says, sounding like it makes her feel uncomfortable.

"Not to worry. This is a temporary passcode. Usually, I can buzz anyone through, but with so much going on tonight, I thought this would simplify matters. When are you heading out?"

"Maybe at six?"

Brian checks his watch—4:30. He heads to his truck and revs it up. "I'm going to take a shower. If you're ready, head on out and visit with Rita. The kids can run off some of their steam before taking the hayride."

"Okay, that sounds really good. These kids are about to drive me nuts asking when we're leaving. I'll get them ready and head over."

"Great! I can't wait." He disconnects the call, feeling like he's ascended to cloud nine.

I hit End on the cellphone and feel like a schoolgirl going on my first, dare I say it, *date*. I know it isn't a date, and lots of people will be there, many of whom I'm sure to know from our small town. But he sounded excited for us to be coming early. I bite my lip and head to the bedroom to change clothes. When I come out, I plop on the couch between the kids.

I put on the biggest frown I can muster. "I talked to Brian, and, well, we won't be going there at seven tonight."

"Oh no!" Mattie cries out, but before Ethan could join in, I spill the beans.

"We'll be going as soon as you two can grab your hats, mittens, and coats!"

In a flash of spinning colors, they are off to their room, grabbing their gear and rushing back into the living room, eyes bright and ready for fun times.

I'm just as eager and zip the corner of my scarf into Mattie's coat, having to peel it out of the zipper as we giggle and hurry to the car, excited for the adventure.

I arrive at the gate and am surprised to see the difference in only a week of not being there. I shrug, remembering Brian had been gone for a week and it really is a good idea to install the extra fencing and gate, especially since he lives out here all alone. I punch in the passcode and drive through.

Both Mattie and Ethan exhale a loud, "Wow!"

It makes me grin. This is the most fun the kids have had in a long time. Actually, their last visit and this one is the only time they've gotten out really, besides my parents' house and the occasional movie.

We follow the winding road, and I catch my breath as I pull into the driveway.

Brian stands there, watching the last shards of sunlight. He wears a cowboy hat and a thick dark brown leather jacket, jeans, and boots. He turns when he notices us and smiles. It's enough to make the snow melt and my heart race. That man sure has an effect on me.

"Brian!" Mattie yells as she struggles to get out of her seat.

Once Ethan is on the ground, they both race up the porch and hug Brian around his legs, causing him to stumble backward into his rocking chair and burst out in laughter.

"Wow, now that is a wonderful hello." He hugs Mattie and ruffles Ethan's hat.

I have climbed the steps by the time Brian crawls from the rocker and tries to dislodge the kids from his arms and legs. "I told you they were eager to come."

"Let's go inside. I need a few volunteers. You see, my sister has been baking cupcakes and—"

Mattie and Ethan repeat "Cupcakes!" over and over.

I can only shake my head; my heart warms seeing them so happy.

Brian opens the door and allows Mattie, Ethan, and me to enter before he closes it and leads us to the kitchen.

I see Rita and walk over to say hello. The kitchen is filled with the banter between Brian and Rita and the giggles of Mattie and Ethan as they so-call *test* the cupcakes to let Rita know they're perfect.

I feel guilty just showing up for the party, when Rita has been baking and cooking enough to feed an army. All the cupcakes are decorated with white icing and are piped along the edges in red or green. Some have bell designs in the center, and some have holly leaves and berries. They are a work of art from the heart. Snooping, I open the lid to the big pot and smell the wonderful aroma of chili cooking. My stomach growls, which Brian doesn't miss.

"How about we all have a small cup of chili, and then we can let Rita know if it needs more seasoning." He grabs paper cups and fills them two-thirds full and brings some plastic wear to the outside table. We sit on the covered porch and eat the chili as the day passes into nightfall. The lights come on all around the porch, initiating the oohs and ahhs. Hundreds of Christmas lights twinkle above us and, as we look across the land, one by one trees light up full of the festive colors. I feel my eyes water. I don't even have a tree up yet. Here, it already feels like Christmas.

I'm lost in the lights, in the beauty all around me, and didn't notice Brian has stood. He leans close to me, his hand so close I feel the warmth radiating toward my hand. I look up and his face is mere inches away. I catch my breath.

"I'm having a glass of mulled wine. Can I bring you one? We have the non-alcoholic version for the youngsters to try."

"Yes, please. That would be wonderful. Let me help. I'll get the ones for Mattie and Ethan to try."

He smiles. His eyes sparkle like the Christmas lights, full of flash and warmth. "Right this way, milady."

It's hard for me to stand; my legs are like overcooked noodles. He had been so close I almost closed my eyes and lifted my chin. It felt like a kiss had been waiting. I clear my throat and follow him into the kitchen. I notice little things now, like how he will lean toward me as we talk and how he sometimes touches my arm when he says something. Can it be he's interested in me? I try shaking the idea from my head. He's just a very kind man and enjoys doing nice things for people. By the time I fill the cups for the children and return to the outside table, Brian's there.

He slips the drink to me and winks. "A little toast, if you please. Rita! Come bring your cup out here and join our toast!"

All stand around the table, lifting cups to the air.

Brian clears his throat. "To our official beginning of the Christmas holidays, to old friends and new, to the memories we make, and to each one of you. Cheers!"

Perhaps it's the Christmas lights gleaming over the snow or the laughter of my children, but I feel Christmas has landed as soft as a bird's feather into my lap. The mulled wine is warm and smooth. The background sounds fade as I meet Brian's gaze. His eyes hold such a warmth that it gives me a rosy glow.

"Look, the guests are arriving." Rita points to approaching headlights.

"And it begins." Brian walks around to the front porch, awaiting the guests.

Nervousness thrums through my blood, causing my heart to race. I draw closer to my children, hoping they will feel comfortable with all the new arrivals. The first to arrive is Luke, the part-time ranch hand. He will ride one of the horses pulling the wagon; Brian will be the other rider.

Brian lets me know he needs to join Luke so they can bring the wagon around to be ready to receive the guests.

Rita asks me to help her set out the pitchers of mulled wine and the one made for the children on the tables on the front porch. She charges Mattie with the paper cups while Ethan brings the napkins.

I can see a steady line from the porch.

It drives up Rita's excitement as she rushes about, ensuring everything was in its place. Once satisfied, she stands at the steps wringing her hands as the first cars arrive. She greets them all enthusiastically, introducing them to me and my children before leading them to the refreshments.

The sound of ringing bells announces the horse-drawn wagon has arrived.

CHAPTER 10

The horses are adorned with bells and red sashes on the sides of their saddles. The wagon shimmers with twinkle lights woven around the sideboards. It amazes me all the trouble Brian and Rita go through to host this special hayride. Mattie and Ethan meet children close to their ages and run back and forth on the porch as all of us adults chat merrily. Each new car arriving revs up the noise level and excitement.

Most of the arrivals have been at the previous hayrides, but some, like me and my family, are new to this adventure and stand on the porch, taking in the trees glowing with Christmas lights; from this vantage point, however, much more can't be seen.

Several children clamber into the wagon and toss hay into the air.

I cautiously help Ethan and Mattie into the wagon and slip the safety rail into place, ensuring none can fall out. Most of the adults gravitate to the wagon to keep a watchful eye on their children as the last few cars navigate to the house.

Brian makes a special point to stop by and talk to me. "I hope you enjoy tonight and make this a holiday tradition." He joins Luke and they mount their horses.

The adults climb into the wagon and find seats and blankets, chatting and pointing out new features across the ranch. Everywhere I glance is illuminated in festive lights. I find myself thrilled to be included in this holiday tradition. It's spectacular. I chuckle to myself, thinking, *We haven't even started caroling or the hayride and I can't see how it could be any more wonderful than this moment.*

Chapter 11

Rita has taken her seat on the front of the wagon next to Shannon, who leads the carolers every year. As the last two cars unload, they join the others in the wagon, quickly getting settled before the wagon starts the journey. Rita is busy sorting through the pages of carols and only looks up once we move.

Shannon bursts out with "Jingle Bells" and everyone joins in.

Rita's voice falters as she watches the last guests board the wagon. Rita spots trouble. The noise is too loud for her to attract Brian's attention. They must have either slipped in as the gate was opening for another guest or came with someone. She darts her gaze at Darci, but Darci is oblivious to the catastrophe in the making. She turns sideways, trying to get Brian's attention, but the noise level is at a fevered pitch.

The wagon bounces around the first curve as gasps and claps of delight fill the air. Along the side of the road are whimsical displays of forest animals painted brightly with spotlights shining around them.

Brian spins on his saddle to look at Darci's reaction, but spots Rita, who mouths, *Samantha*. He sees her sitting in the back of the wagon, talking with Meredith, an old friend of theirs.

His jaw clenches tight as he turns back in his saddle. He berates himself for his lack of calling everyone to warn them against bringing Samantha onto the property.

That's unfair. My friends shouldn't be drawn into my personal problems. He knows it's Samantha's attempt to worm her way back into his life. And now, she's making it public—in front of Darci. He has to figure out a way to diffuse the situation before it turns bad. He can't very well stop the ride and throw her out. This night is for everyone, and most have looked forward to the festivities since last year.

I glance at everyone in the wagon having fun. Mattie and Ethan are thrilled to be around so many other kids on the hayride. They sing along with the carolers, even songs they don't know by heart. It makes my spirit fly as they giggle when they get the words incorrect. These are memories they will long carry. When I look at Rita, I think she looks pale, as if the work of the day has finally caught up with her.

Rita catches me looking and pats the spot next to her.

With a smile, I thread through the children and plop next to Rita and lean over. "Are you feeling all right? You look a little pale. Can I get you anything?"

"No, sugar. I'm okay, just a bit startled."

"What startled you? The children?"

"No, dear. They're fine, a sheer joy to watch them having fun. I-I really don't know how to say this, and I don't want it to ruin your evening."

I tilt my head with brows furrowed in puzzlement. "I don't understand. I'm having a great time."

Rita's fingers pull at the edges of the blanket across her lap. She glances over her shoulder at her brother, but he's facing forward as he slowly pulls the wagon along the path. "Someone is here who wasn't invited."

"Oh, Rita. From what I know of Brian, he won't mind. He seems to be very giving."

"He is a wonderful man, and you're right. Most of the time, he'd go with the flow. *Come one, come all*, sort of thing. This is different. His … old flame is here with her son."

I catch my breath. Someone Brian had been involved with just showed up on her own? Who would do that, and why? I hardly have time to think about it further when Mattie approaches me to introduce a new friend.

"Mommy, this is Billy. He says he used to live here with Brian and his mommy." She turns and points at a lady talking to another woman next to her. "He says his Papa Brian got him all these animals on the ranch."

My chest hurts, like it will cave in. "Hi, Billy. It's nice to meet you."

"Nice to meet you too," he says with a smile. "I've been on a lot of these hayrides. They're fun."

"They sure are, Billy. We're having the best time."

"Hi, Miss Rita. Do you remember me? I bet I've grown a lot since you've seen me."

"Hello, Billy. Why yes, you've grown by leaps and bounds," Rita replies.

Mattie loses interest in the adults and returns to Ethan. Billy follows.

I notice Rita's cheeks are red as she reaches out and squeezes my hand. We sit in an uncomfortable silence as my mind pulls away in thought. I'm irritated because I thought Brian was interested in me; although, we only shared a pizza that one time and just last week had our first hayride. It isn't like we are dating or anything. I shake my head at my own folly. He's only being the kind man he is—nothing more. It doesn't hurt any less, telling myself these things. It doesn't erase the hope of becoming closer to him; it just sets them on a slow burn, watching them disintegrate before my eyes. The most telling of all is when Billy called

Brian *Papa* Brian. No wonder he's so good with children. He has one of his own.

The hayride completes its circle and pulls across from the house where a bonfire is ready to be lit.

Luke jumps down and removes the safety boards at the back of the wagon and sets the bonfire ablaze.

Billy grabs his mom's arm and helps her down, and they walk to where Brian is dismounting his horse. "Surprise!" Billy yells as he lunges forward to hug Brian.

I jump down and help Ethan and Mattie to the ground and wander toward the fire. Around the bonfire are many curved cedar benches, highly glossed with a clear coat of lacquer. Some chairs sit between the curved benches circling the fire.

Everyone gathers close and cheers the roaring flames.

Rita distributes the skewers and hot dogs, hot cocoa, and napkins.

I suddenly feel all alone. I look around and see Billy already at the fire, roasting a hot dog, but his mother and Brian aren't anywhere to be seen. I want to leave, but this isn't only for myself; it's for my children, and they are still having a good time. I head to the long tables holding the pot of chili, bowls, chips, and other goodies. I ladle some chili into a bowl and spoon in bites of the warmth as I keep an eye on the kids. This is another first—roasting their own hot dogs.

Mattie holds two skewers, taking such good care of her brother. They come up to me to have them slipped into the buns and hand their skewers to Luke. They make me so proud.

I motion for them to sit on the bench and bring them a cup of hot chocolate to go with their hot dogs. I hear approaching footsteps behind me.

"Hi, Brian! This is so much fun," Mattie says between bites of hot dog.

"I'm glad you're having great fun. I'd like to introduce everyone to Samantha. I hear you've met Billy. Samantha is an old friend who stopped by, but she can't stay long. Right, Samantha?" Brian says with a raised brow.

"Hello, everyone. Yes, Billy and I caught a ride with a friend and, unfortunately, we have to cut the evening short."

I stand and extend my hand. "Hello, Samantha. I'm Darci."

There is a long pause before Samantha shakes it. "Hi. Forgive us, but I need to find Billy and get him ready to head out." She turns to hug Brian, but he steps backward. "So … I guess this is goodnight?" She flashes him a coy pout.

"No, Samantha. This is goodbye." He walks away from her and joins Rita and Luke in the line, serving the food.

I don't know what happened, but I can tell it isn't at all what Samantha had in mind. She practically drags Billy from the fireside as he tries to engulf the last of his hot dog. It twists my heart to see him pulled away from the party and from the one he calls *Papa* Brian. I know there has to be much more to this story than I know, but it isn't any of my business. Not anymore, and I aim to keep it that way.

Mattie and Ethan finish their hot dogs and ask if they can make another one.

I smile. "Sure. Enjoy the night." No sense in spoiling the evening for everyone; in fact, I'm glad everything came out the way it did before I found myself attached to the crazy idea that Brian might be interested in me. I don't want my children to think of Brian as someone who will be in their lives for the long run.

It's only after most of the guests are in the process of eating that Brian slips away and stands in front of me, taking advantage that Mattie and Ethan are with the other children in line for cupcakes. "Darci, do you have a moment?"

I see the tension on his face. "Sure. What's up?"

"Walk with me?"

I nod and follow him to the far side of the wagon.

"Tonight didn't turn out how I had imagined. I want to fill you in on the things you don't know."

"Brian, no. I get it. It's fine." I turn to walk away, but he catches my arm and stops me.

"No, it isn't *fine*. It's a mess—or at least one that Samantha is hoping to make a mess. Look. I won't deny we were an item once, but that was years ago. I fell in love with her and Billy and let them into my life. I thought it was love, but it wasn't. I was only one of several men she used and tired of then move on to the next one. I hate it for Billy, but I can't change things. It took me years to become myself again, and there is no room in my life for them, not even for Billy, because Samantha will use him as her pawn."

My jaw drops. "That's a horrible thing to say."

He sighs. "I know it is, and I'm sorry it sounds cruel, but it's the truth. You just don't know Samantha like I do, like Rita does, or anyone who knows the whole story. The best thing Samantha did for me was leave me a note saying goodbye. She had grown bored of the quiet life, the country life, and had to go to the big city with bright lights and fun. I've not heard from her before today."

"I'm sorry, Brian. I know you must hurt." I shuffle on my feet, looking down. "I wanted to let you know, even with the … well, the hayride and bonfire were a hit. The kids will have this as a favorite memory, so thank you." I walk away from him.

"No, Darci," he says as he runs in front of me and stops. "I wanted this to make a special memory for *you*, something to build on and add to." He looks at his shaking hands. "It's crazy, trust me, I know. We've only known each other for a few weeks, but I want to know you more. I think you feel something too. You make the colors brighter, the stars shine. Your laughter is a bird's flight across my soul. Please don't let Samantha's interruption take those things from me."

I stand there, looking at the ground, not trusting myself to look into his eyes. The fear of trusting him, the fear of exposing myself to pain, courses through my veins. I want to run. Thoughts crash into themselves. I bite my lower lip and raise my eyes to meet his. “I’m sorry, Brian. I just can’t. I don’t want to start something and watch my children go through what Billy must be going through. I’m … I’m sorry.”

I gather Mattie and Ethan, take us to the car, and buckle them into their seats. I keep the talk lively, hearing all the wonderful moments we experienced during the hayride and bonfire. I let them talk and talk as I drive home. They are fast asleep by the time I pull into the parking lot. I rouse them enough to get them inside and dressed for bed, then I sit on the couch and let the tears of *what could have been* flow.

CHAPTER 12

The following week is hectic, but it suits me just fine—at least I've been too busy to think about Brian. Mom picked up the kids from daycare and school and kept them until I finished with errands. I still have a tree to buy and presents to get and wrap before Mattie and Ethan can find them in the small apartment.

Wednesday, I receive a call from the photo department that my portraits are ready. I've forgotten all about them, with the recent turn of events. Those pictures are the ones with Mattie and Ethan on the ponies. I know they will be thrilled to have pictures of themselves on the ponies, but it worries me they might want to go back to see Brian, and I really don't want to have that discussion. I shrug. *Maybe by Christmas, it will be better, and they will only remember the fun time they had.*

All the loose ends to tie up before the Christmas Extravaganza keep me busy until the morning of the event. I need to show I can handle the job, and this is the biggest event of the year. Everything has to go off without a hitch. Since I will have to make myself available to all the vendors during the hours they are there, my parents volunteer to keep the children and bring them while I work.

I try to keep on the opposite side of the park from where the Santa's booth is set up because I know Brian will be staged close by. It's only been a week, but I don't feel up to running into him.

It's busy enough; I shouldn't have to worry. It looks as if the whole town has shown up, and that lifts my heart.

There are craft booths and face painting stations, storytelling in the gazebo decked out in festive bows, lots of holiday decorations to be bought, and even more homemade goodies to buy. I'm proud of myself, watching all the people enjoying the event.

The intercom buzzes with static, then a voice announces a little girl is lost and looking for her mother at Santa's booth.

I hurry across the park to wait with the little girl. Arriving at Santa's booth, I see a child who looks to be a bit older than Ethan. I hold one of the little girl's hands, a huge cotton candy dangling in her other.

Her mother, frantic, runs up close to tears. "You've found her! Lisa, where did you go? I turned around, and you disappeared."

"I took my tickets and bought cotton candy. Want some?"

The mother thanks me for finding her and keeping her safe, then walks off hand in hand with her daughter before I can explain I didn't find her, but stayed with her to keep her company as we waited.

I glance at the reindeer area filled with children feeding them.

Brian's back is turned to me, but Samantha and Billy are in plain sight.

Samantha spots me and produces a huge smile. It doesn't take a genius to know they are back together, so I hurry away and stay on the far end of the park.

The booths start breaking down at five o'clock, and by six most have left the park. Mattie and Ethan left with my parents hours ago. I still have to ensure the cleanup crew are prepared to remove benches and leftover trash.

I feel a tap on my shoulder and turn around. I thought it might be Brian. I'm wrong.

Samantha stands there as pretty as you please, smiling like she swallowed a whole cat.

"Hi, Samantha," I say.

"I saw you over here and just wanted to say hello. We're about to leave and head to the ranch. It was a lovely event. I heard you were in charge of it this year." Her smug look makes my stomach boil.

"Thank you. I'm glad you enjoyed it. I'm sorry, I really must run. I'm needed over there." I point at a crew disassembling the benches by the gazebo.

"See ya around," Samantha purrs.

Not if I can help it. I fish my keys from my pocket and scurry to the car. I'm so done here. Driving around the streets, I let my blood pressure return to normal before I go to my parents' house.

They gush about how well the event had gone.

"Better than previous years," my dad proudly states.

I make small talk, then gather Mattie and Ethan to go home and try not to think of Samantha and Brian together at the cabin

CHAPTER 13

Rita has tried to talk to me several times since the hayride, but I always push her away, finally telling her I don't want to hear another word about her brother. So, when I go to my apartment after the event, all Rita can do is stand at her window and sadly shake her head.

We have two different Christmas parties that week, both for the children, but it helps fill the week with happy moments. Christmas morning is right around the corner and we have planned to have our Christmas first at our place, then we will go to my parents afterward and stay for my mother's famous Christmas meal. I sigh, thankful my parents are near, because frankly, I don't have the energy or desire to make a Christmas meal with all the trimmings, and the children deserve to have that.

It snowed overnight. When the kids wake up, they come shouting into my room. "Mommy, Mommy! Come look! Santa was here!"

I stumble out of bed and into the living room where Mattie stands next to a teal-colored bicycle, and Ethan removes the cars from his toy car garage to make them *zoom* in his hands. They tear through their stockings and apples, oranges, and nuts pour out, as well as brightly covered chocolate candies. My heart is thankful to see them so happy.

My doorbell rings and I answer it by opening the door, but leaving the chain across the lock.

"Merry Christmas, Darci. I know you're busy with the children." Rita laughs. "I could hear them over at my place."

"I'm sorry if they woke you. I'll have them tone it down a notch."

"No, don't worry about it. I just stopped by to give you this card. Merry Christmas." She slides the card through the opening and hurries to her apartment.

Smiling, I close the door, tear open the envelope, and gasp seeing a beautiful card of the cabin with the frozen pond in front.

> *Dear Darci,*
>
> *Merry Christmas to you and yours. I'm doing my best to give you space, but it's difficult. I wish I could have talked to you at the Christmas Extravaganza. You seemed to be overly busy and never made it over to the reindeer, or maybe that was your plan. It's just as well. Samantha and Billy showed up and had to follow me to the ranch. They had left in such a hurry previously that I stored their things in one of the sheds. Anyway, at last I have all their things gone, and they are on their way back to the city lights and someone she once knew. Good riddance.*
>
> *I write all this to ask you if the gift I chose for Mattie and Ethan is all right. You see, Mattie fell in love with Bella, and I think it was the same for Ethan and Dark Knight. After Mattie was so sad about me giving them away, I decided to keep them and give them as presents to her and her brother. The reason I ask you is I know they have no place for the ponies, and it means they would want to come out and ride them at the ranch. Please understand I thought of this before Samantha showed up, and, well, you decided you didn't want to further our relationship. This isn't a ploy. I'm not that kind of man. It's a heartfelt gift. I won't even say a word about it if you choose to decline the gift. But, if you decide they can have the ponies, I'll work with any decision on how they can come ride. If*

you prefer, you can let Rita know whether or not the ponies are theirs.
I hope everyone has a Merry Christmas. You are in my thoughts.
Always, Brian

I read the card multiple times, shaking my head in disbelief. *That Samantha! She led me to believe she had moved in with Brian, and she did it on purpose, knowing she was only going there to pick up their belongings. Brian has been honest all along.* The tears freely flow as I clasp a hand over my mouth.

It suddenly grows quiet in the apartment. I look down to see Ethan's bottom lip trembling, and Mattie has stopped admiring her new bike.

"Mommy, what's wrong?" Ethan asks, close to tears himself.

I sit on the floor, crying and laughing, and scoop him into my lap. "Come here, Mattie. It's a Christmas card. What do you see?"

"It's Brian's ranch! Look how beautiful it is." Mattie's fingers trail over the picture.

"Sweetie, do Mommy a favor and grab those two presents by the wall. Yes, those, honey. The flat ones." I wait for Mattie to bring them back.

"This one is for Ethan, and the other one has my name on it."

"Okay, you can both open them." I lean back to the sound of them shredding paper.

"Oh, look! It's me on Bella." She hugs it close to her chest.

"I have one with Dark Knight. I loved that pony. Thank you, Mommy. Now I'll always remember him." He hugs me, sniffling.

"That is only part one of your gift."

They both look up in surprise.

"The reason Mommy was crying is because of the wonderful gift in store for you both. You see, Brian saw how much you both loved those ponies, and he's given them to you as your Christmas present."

Mattie falls to the ground in tears, hugging her picture. When she looks up, she says, “I thought he said he was giving them away.”

I nod with tears in my eyes. “Yes, but he saw how much you both loved them and kept them to surprise you for Christmas. He knows we don’t have a place to keep them, so he’ll keep them at the ranch, and you can ride them, brush them, and feed them whenever you want.”

“We can? Really? Ethan! We have our own ponies! Mommy, can we go there right now?”

“Oh, honey, I bet Brian isn’t even awake yet.”

“He’s awake,” she says, nodding. “You forget, he has a whole ranch to take care of. Please, Mommy?”

“I’ll tell you what—you both get clothes on, and I’ll get changed. Then we’ll see if he’s awake. If so, we’ll stop by before going to Granny and Grandpa’s. How’s that sound?”

“Yay!” they shout, and I hurry to throw on a Christmas sweater and jeans.

Once they’re ready, I dial his number.

He answers on the first ring. “Hello?”

“Hello, Brian. This is Darci. Rita’s next-door neighbor. The one you came and fixed the tire for.”

Hearing his laughter makes me laugh as my tears still flow. “Hello, Darci, Rita’s next-door neighbor, the one I came and fixed the tire for. Merry Christmas.”

“Merry Christmas, Brian.”

CHAPTER 14

I try to hold back the tears pouring down my face. "Mattie and Ethan love their Christmas gifts. They are asking to come over before we go to their grandparents' house for Christmas. Could I bring them by to see the ponies?"

"Please do. I'm headed out to the barns now to start the feeding. And Darci?"

"Yes?"

"Thank you for letting them have the presents."

"Thank you for being so thoughtful and kind. They love those ponies. I gave them the pictures I took of them riding them at your ranch. Then I received your card. I was in tears. This has to be their best Christmas ever—and mine, too."

The phone grows quiet for a moment. "So, you'll be at the grandparents' for Christmas?"

"Yes, we'll do the Christmas present exchange and have a wonderful meal that my mom so graciously prepared for us. We'll head back home early afternoon. Why?"

"That would work out well. You see, Rita will be cooking up a feast for us today. We'll be having Christmas dinner around six tonight and then, a little ride around the ranch. I'd love it if you would join us."

"We accept!" My voice explodes over the phone and is met with Brian's good-natured chuckle.

"Wonderful. I'm planning on a winter wonderland that I think you, as well as the children, will enjoy."

"Please, don't go to all that trouble for us. It will be more than enough just to enjoy the company and the landscape." I'm still feeling guilty over imagining the worst of him and now he is showing me just how truly kind he is.

"I wish I could say it was all for you, but the truth is Christmas brings out the little kid in me. I had planned on doing this little wonderland anyway. Rita gets such a kick out of what I do each year. I can't let her down."

I chuckle. "You are an amazing brother." I want to say and man, but I hold back. As it is, things between Brian and I are going a bit too fast and that's what almost tore us apart. I want to take time to really get to know him.

"When do you think Mattie and Ethan will be ready to come out?"

"Are you kidding me? They're the ones that told me to call you this early. Mattie said you would be awake because of all the animals you care for."

He laughs again. "She was right. I've been up for a few hours already and well, I had high hopes that I'd hear from you."

"We'll be there in thirty minutes?"

"Perfect! I'll see you soon. Oh, and the gate code today is 12-25-21."

"So creative." I try to smother my laugh, but it comes out anyway.

"Genius, right? Stop at the house when you get here. I'd like you to see the transformation of the house."

"Be there in a bit and we're looking forward to it. Thank you, Brian." I hang up before I have another fit of tears. Even after all I put him through, he still is so sweet. A thought flashes in my mind. I didn't get him a present! My mind races. Then I think about of the neck scarf I just completed in blue and grey. Yes, that would be perfect for him. I smile heading to my bedroom to change and wrap the scarf.

Between all the jumping up and down and squirming, I've got warm clothes on Mattie and Ethan and out the door we go. I see Rita peering out her window and I wave her to the door.

"Thank you for delivering the card. We are on our way to see the ponies."

Rita clasps her hands together and grins like a cat swallowing a bird. "I'm so happy to hear it!"

"We'll be going over to my parents' afterwards and enjoying Christmas morning with them and the noon-day Christmas meal. Brian invited us over for dinner tonight since he said you'll be cooking up a storm."

"That's great news. I can't wait for you to join us. He thinks I go over the top each Christmas, but it is really him. I'm eager to see what he has planned this year. Merry Christmas, Darci. This day just keep getting better and better."

I grin and wave goodbye as I rush the kids out to the Volvo. The snow lightly falls around us, adding to the beauty of the sunrise, as if golden coins rain down. If I had wished for a perfect Christmas, it would have to be this one.

It doesn't take long to arrive at Brian's house. Just like the card he sent us, it is picturesque. Snow has gathered in rounded mounds on the tops of the fence posts and the tree limbs, softening everything in sight. Ethan bounces in his car seat, bubbling over with joy. And Mattie? Bless her heart, she feels things as deeply as I do, and tender tears run down her cheek.

"I know what. Let's sing Jingle Bells as loud as we can so Brian will hear us signing as we pull up to the cabin." I figure it will help us stop crying and look more cheerful when we arrive. It works. Mattie belts out the song to the capacity of her lungs. I laugh and join in as Ethan sings and bounces to the rhythm. I can hardly put the car into Park when Brian steps out to the porch wearing faded jeans, a red sweater, and an open, bulky tan coat.

"Merry Christmas one and all!" He chuckles as he sees me trying to unlatch the belt over Mattie's car seat and help her down. I didn't noticed Brian left the porch until the other car door opens and he's helping Ethan out of his car seat. They're all over him like glue, hugging and thanking him.

"When can we see our ponies?" Mattie is trying to drag Brian to the barns.

"After we go inside for a minute. I want you to see the Christmas tree and decorations." Brian grabs Mattie's hand as I scoop Ethan up to navigate up the porch.

Opening the door, we cross the threshold to see the tree full of lights, ornaments, and cookies tied with bows dotting the branches. "We'll nibble on those cookies later, but I just pulled out these obey-gooey cinnamon buns from the oven and covered them with frosting. Anyone want one?"

We all say 'me!' as he dishes out rolls onto festive Christmas tree plates and we sit at the table to enjoy them. Mattie waves behind me towards the stairs and I feel my stomach drop. All I could think of is… Samantha.

"Merry Christmas, Mom and Dad. You're just in time for some cinnamon rolls. This is Darci and her two children, Mattie and Ethan. The one's I told you I gave the ponies to."

By the time I turn to see his parents coming down the stairs, his mother winks and says, "Oh! How lovely to see you all. Brian has told us so much about you."

I feel my mouth drop to my plate. I try to recover and stand up. "Hi. I hope we didn't wake you." I walk over to give them a handshake and realize I have icing all over my fingers. His mother laughs.

"I'll just give you a quick hug so you can go back and enjoy those wonderful smelling rolls. Come, George. I'll get us each one if you'll pour us some coffee."

I want to hide. I didn't know Brian's parents were here. *Gaw, I'm such a lame-o. Of course they would come to be with their family on Christmas day. How could I have been so dense? And here we are intruding on family time.* I crawl back into my chair and down the coffee in front of me. Mattie and Ethan devour their rolls and are hastily trying to wipe the icing onto their napkins.

"Brian, before you go to the barns, can we give Mattie and Ethan their presents?" his mother asks with cheeks nearly as red as Santa's.

Oh my god... I'm going to die! His parents have presents for my children? Why would they do that for strangers? I feel doubly worse. I don't have anything to give them. Mattie's question pulls me out of my thoughts.

"Can we, Mommy?" Mattie asks shrilly.

"Oh goodness. I don't know what to say. We've only just met and I didn't know you would be here. I'm so unprepared and I'm used to being on the ball—"

His mother has Brian's contagious laughter. "Oh, please. You'll make me cry. Brian said you had a way of talking that could rev up from zero to ninety in nothing flat. The presents are companion presents for what Brian already gave them. I hope you don't mind. I just couldn't resist."

George raises his eyebrows and shakes his head. "I can attest to that. She couldn't resist. One of the things I love dearly about my darling Connie is her nature of giving."

Connie, her name is Connie, I repeat to myself. "I suppose it's okay, Mattie."

Connie claps her hands together in as much delight as the children wear on their faces. She shuffles over to the Christmas tree and pulls out one long box and one square box, handing them to Mattie and Ethan. I stand next to Brian and glance up at him. He's wearing a million-dollar smile. I'm gobsmacked. I—I don't even know how to act.

"Look, Mommy, look!" Mattie pulls this long, red cape out of the box.

"It's a riding cape, Mattie. When you take Bella out for a ride, it will keep you warm," Connie answers, dabbing a tissue to her eyes.

"Oh my! That is beautiful. Thank you so much for giving that to Mattie." I feel the heat of tears building in the corner of my eyes.

"Look at me, Mommy! I got a cowboy hat and a jacket. Hey, it looks like your jacket, Brian, 'cept it's shrunk down," Ethan says, trying to get his arms through the coat sleeves.

We all start laughing and that helps me feel a bit better of our intrusion. "Thank you for their gifts. You both are too kind," I manage to blurt out.

"Nonsense, dear. These are practical gifts for horse riders." She winks, but follows up with a beaming smile.

I help Ethan into his new leather jacket and cowboy hat as Mattie spins in circles watching her cape fly. When I turn to look at Connie, she has her hands covering her mouth, which I am sure is hiding her smile. Her eyes are glistening.

"Really, I can't thank you enough for the considerate gifts." I splay my hands out trying to convey my heartfelt thanks.

Mattie runs over to Connie and wraps her arms around her knees. "Thank you! I can't wait to wear it when I ride Bella."

"Speaking of Bella, we better get you two down to the barn to feed her and Dark Knight. They'll be getting hungry about now," Brian says, guiding us to the door.

"It was so nice meeting you both," I say.

"It's our pleasure to meet all of you. I hope we see you again soon," Connie answers, still dewy-eyed.

Brian grins and answers, "They've agreed to join us tonight for dinner after they have their Christmas at their grandparents' house."

"Wonderful, we'll see you then." Connie and George wave as we leave the house.

We walk through the pristine snow, adding our footprints. I love the way the snow crunches underfoot. Something about the footprints warm me up inside, making me feel as if we belong here. I can't help but turn my head to look at the line of footprints in the snow. Brian's, Mattie's, Ethan's, and mine. The snow covers all the past history and creates a clean, blank slate for us to fill. A smile radiates from within.

At the barn, Mattie and Ethan are busy pulling Brian along to reach their ponies. I catch my breath when we reach the ponies' stalls. Each one is festooned with saddles and a swag of evergreen draped over their necks with pretty red bows and bells. I grab my phone and take several pictures before I have to put it away and help Mattie grab her bucket to feed Bella. Brian takes Ethan by the hand to Dark Knight, who is already whinnying for his food. The sound of music fills my ears—the sound of my children's bubbling laughter and I can't get enough of it.

After feeding the ponies, I take Mattie's hand and lift her up into her seat as Brian rustles Ethan into his. By the time I scootch into my driver's seat, Brian is standing at my door. I forgot that I have his wrapped present in my front seat. Rolling the window down, I grin and hand him the wrapped package.

"What is this?" He looks perplexed as he turns the package from front to back.

"Merry Christmas, Brian. It's just a little something from me—from us."

He tears the paper open and a smile spreads over his face. "I love it! My favorite colors, too." He wraps it around his neck, running a hand down the length of it. "When did you have time to shop for me today?"

"I didn't. I made it." I feel my cheeks blush as the surprise registers on his face.

He leans in and places a soft kiss on my cheek and lingers. "Thank you," he whispers close to my ear. I can't help it, I shiver from head to toes. "I better let you raise your window before you freeze. I'll see you soon." He backs away from the car, still running a hand over the knitted scarf.

Freeze? I'm about to melt, I want to say. Instead I wave and start down the road, constantly watching my rearview mirror. He stands in the road, one hand in a pocket, the other one stroking the neck scarf. I swear he is going to make me cry, standing there like that, as if that is the best present he's ever received. All I want to do is get to my parents' place, let the kids have their time with Granny and Grandpa, then eat and get back to Brian. I know that's not fair, so I'll try to slow down once we get there, but it will be hard.

CHAPTER 15

Mom hears us as I pull in and has the door open and ready. I hardly get Mattie out of the car when she rushes to her Granny and hugs her tight. As soon as Ethan is released, it's an encore performance. I make it up to the porch to hear Ethan telling her where his new coat and hat came from.

She raises an eyebrow to me as she hustles us all into the warmth of the house. I know she'll ask soon enough, but in the meantime I head to the tree and dig out the presents I brought over earlier for them from us. Let the festivities begin! Mom grabs the presents for me and Mattie and Ethan and Dad distribute the rest. The noise level is through the roof with the kids showing off one present after another. I stop for a moment and realize how much my life has changed in the last few years. Tears threaten to leak as I watch the joy in this room and how much love I feel pulsating around me. I move over to my mom and wrap my arm around her as we watch the children laugh and play. This is all I want for them, to feel the same love I had growing up and for that matter, still do.

Christmas music plays along with the movies on the Christmas channel. Glancing outside, there are still a few flurries drifting down, just enough to add to the holiday feel without worrying about travel plans. A perfect Christmas.

Mom heads toward the kitchen and I follow. The aroma in here is killing me. Looking at the center island with its twinkle lights and garland streaming around it and the surface is covered in all of my favorites, I wonder how am I going to eat some of everything and still be able to eat at Brian's house.

"So, who are these mysterious people who gave our grandchildren such extravagant presents? This is the first I've heard of them."

"I just met them…" Before I can get another word out, mom interrupts. Her eyes have grown two sizes and threaten to pop off her face.

"What? You just met these people and they had presents that look the perfect size for both of your children? Honey, I think I need to hear *all* about this," she says, topping off her cup of coffee.

"Do you remember me mentioning Brian, the guy who brought the reindeer to the Christmas Extravaganza? No? Well, it's all been rather sudden. I had to go to his cabin to get him to sign the paperwork to authorize him bringing them and taking part in the event since he was going to be out of town a week. Anyway, long story cut down, he invited us to a hayride the following week. Mom, he is really nice and *whew*, is he ever good looking."

"Who exactly is this Brian? He lives here? What is his last name?" Mom has her motherly instincts in overdrive.

"His name is Brian Walters and it was his parents that gave the gifts to Mattie and Ethan. Gosh, mom, there is so much to tell to catch you up on things."

"You just talk away while I baste this ham and stir the pots. I'm all ears." I see the twinkle in her eyes.

I laugh and hug her. It's nice to be able to share something with her besides work. I tell her most everything about Brian, but I leave out telling her anything about Samantha and Billy. Just the quick thought of them is enough to leave a sour taste in my mouth.

"So, he doesn't work?" Mom's forehead looks like a road map.

"Oh, he does…sort of. He sold a business and now he has all sorts of animals. He takes them to children's parties, events, and even some of the PSTD ranches with his horses to help them with rehabilitating. That is what he was going to do when I went to the cabin to get the papers signed for the Christmas event."

"And how is it that his parents came to know my grandchildren and buy them presents?"

"Uh, I really don't know yet. We were just stopping by the cabin this morning so the kids to feed their ponies." A lid slips out of her hands and clangs on the stovetop.

"What? Who got them *ponies*?" Her eyes are enormous.

"Mom! It's all confusing to tell this way. Brian gave them the ponies because when we went there, they rode them and fell in love with them. He was talking and telling us he was donating the ponies they rode to a place for others to enjoy, and well, the kids just about cried. You know how Mattie is with animals—well she hit a soft spot in Brian. He kept them to surprise the kids with them for Christmas."

"But Darci, you live in an apartment."

"I know, mom, but he's letting them keep the ponies at the cabin and come ride or feed them anytime they want."

"Uh huh." She gives me this 'mom' look and I know what she's thinking.

"It isn't like that."

"Like what, Darci? Like a convenient way to have you over to his cabin frequently? And now, his parents, who you say you just met, had presents for them? I don't understand any of this." Instead of wringing her hands, she's briskly rubbing her hands down the front of her apron.

I bite the corner of my lip, thinking. "I can't answer as to why they had presents for Mattie and Ethan. I mean, I didn't know until today that I would ever see Brian again." *Oh no!* my brain flashed.

Mom halts stirring the gravy, knocks the spoon on the side of the pan and stands with both fists bunched up on the sides of her apron. "Who are these people? Are they mixed up in some crazy cult or something?"

I can't help it and burst into laughter. "Mom, seriously? They are simply kind and giving people. I know it seems foreign to us, especially after the way my ex behaved, but they are genuine. Please mom, don't judge them so harshly for being kind. After all, it *is* the Christmas season."

She exhales deeply and gives a quick nod. "I guess I may be worrying too much for my only daughter. It's just that I love you so much, and know what you've gone through. You finally have your life where it's making sense to you and your children, *my* grandchildren, are happier than ever before."

"I know, mom. I love you, too. Don't worry, everything is okay." Even I know what I'm saying is just noise in the wind when speaking to my mom.

After mom slides several dishes into the oven to stay warm, we shuffle through piles of discarded Christmas wrappings and join the family in the living room. Dad has a cheesy grin on his face and I wonder what is going through his mind. I don't have to wonder for long.

"Mother, Mattie has invited us to go see their new ponies. Isn't that nice? I told her it wouldn't be proper to go today, as this is a special day for families to be together, even though they'll be going out tonight to have dinner at Brian's house."

I feel it. It's that rising heat that always attaches itself to my face when I'm embarrassed.

"However, since she's so excited over their ponies I let her know we would love to go see them, say tomorrow? What do you think?"

My mom has a grin like a cat. "What a lovely idea. Oh, what fun that will be. Of course, we'll go out to see their new ponies!"

I'm doomed. Literally doomed. I can only imagine the interrogation my parents will put Brian through.

Mom turns to me and says, "Darci, love, please let Brian know we'll stop by tomorrow when you take the kids out to feed the ponies, to see their wonderful gifts. I wouldn't want him to think we're coming out there snooping on him." She has the nerve to bat her eyes at me.

"Fine, mom. You guys can follow us out there when we go. I'm sure Brian will be delighted to meet you." I have visions of a shotgun wedding playing through my head.

The next few hours pass with playing games like Candyland and Chutes and Ladders while *Rudolph the Red Nosed Reindeer* plays on the television. I finally feel the tension of the previous discussion melt when mom tells us it's time to eat. Well, she doesn't say it exactly like that…

"Come on, let's go eat all of this deliciousness, so Darci and the grandkids can go see Brian and his parents."

Have you ever rolled your eyes so hard they hit the back of your skull? It can happen. Trust me on this.

I linger and enjoy each bite, raving how she has outdone herself with this wonderful meal. I mean every word, too. Mom, with a gleam in her eyes, loads up the dessert plates, especially for the kids. Without her even having to say it, I know what her retort will be. *'What? You know they'll burn off all that sugar once you get to Bri-an's.'* Complete with his name drawn out to linger long after her words end.

We load up the car with as much of the presents as we can, and I promise to get the rest tomorrow when we go out to feed the ponies. Mom simply grins. The contents in my stomach flip like pancakes. I can't wait to get home, unload the car, and hope for an hour nap before rounding up the kids and heading to Brian's.

CHAPTER 16

After an hour and a half snooze, I awake to the startling revelation that I have no gifts to bring Brian's parents. It's rather embarrassing, as they have gone to such trouble to give gifts to Mattie and Ethan. Having just met them, I have no idea of what they would like and I'm clueless on what to do. I know it isn't necessary to bring them gifts but…their kindness to my children overwhelms me.

I've got it! Rustling the children into the living room, I put Mattie's cape on her and Ethan's cowboy hat and leather jacket on him. A grin splits their facesas they stand in front of the Christmas tree. A few snaps from my phone and I'm ready for the printer. They turn out gorgeous! Cringing, I know I don't have any extra picture frames, so I go on a scavenger hunt through the apartment looking for frames to fit. At last, I find two matching frames, remove the pictures in them, and dust them off and insert the new pictures. I tape the already spent bows from under the Christmas tree to each corner. Voila! Presents to bring to Brian's house. The pictures look better than any shopping mall photo session and I hope it will give them a smile over the kind gifts they gave.

The sun is setting fast as I get the kids situated in the car. I look around our apartment complex and hear all the giddy laughter of children at play. This has already been the best Christmas in memory. I jump into the driver's seat, roaring the Volvo to life.

Every time I pull onto Brian's road, I'm mesmerized by its scenic quality. An artist couldn't paint a picture to compare with the beauty I hold in my eyes. I use the gate code to enter and wait for the gate to lock behind us before driving any further. I get a shiver as I recall the night *Samantha* just showed up for the hayride and drove a wedge between Brian and myself. I'm not looking for a repeat performance tonight. I try to shake off the spoilt moment, and it doesn't take long. The snow glistens like thousands of diamonds cast across the ground. The pond is iced over and catches the sunset on its surface. Shaken out of the moment, Mattie starts singing, this time to "Silent Night," and I find it perfect for the drive.

As we round the bend in the road, the cabin comes into view. It's breathtaking. The snow has mounded up on the ends of the logs, garland is wrapped around each post, and the wrap-around porch just beckons all visitors to it. My heart is full. There isn't any other place I would wish to be than where I am right now. I hardly have time to turn off the ignition before Brian, Rita and their parents come out to the porch. Each one is laughing and full of cheer. Brian jumps down and hurries to Ethan's door as I get Mattie out of her seat. Then it hits me like a snowball from out of nowhere. They are all wearing those funny Christmas sweaters! Each one a bit more ridiculously festive than the last. Brian has even put away his cowboy hat in favor of a Santa's hat! I'm grinning and I wish I would have dug out one of my Christmas sweaters for the occasion.

Out of the corner of my eye I see Brian swooshing Ethan through the air before gently placing him on the porch. Mattie plows into the back of his legs, toppling him and Ethan and sending Rita backwards, but she is saved by her dad propping her up by her elbows.

"Mattie!" She swivels her head at the tone of my voice.

"Sorry, Mommy. I didn't know I would knock them out."

Brian has a fit of laughter as he slaps the snow from his legs. "It's knocked me down, not out, Mattie. I'd hate for the rumor to get started that a young lady knocked me out on Christmas day."

I can only shake my head. Brian never seems to get bothered by their antics, but I shake a finger at Mattie and remind her to be more careful.

Rita meets me at the porch and hands me a mug of mulled wine, elbowing me and adding a wink. "Merry Christmas, neighbor. Have a mug or two and you'll fit right in with the rest of our silliness." My heart is near exploding by being included for this wonderful occasion.

Connie and George bring out a mug of cocoa for each of the kids and call for a toast. "In honor of family being pulled together for another year and meeting new friends, Merry Christmas!"

Rounds of *Merry Christmas* fill the air. I always enjoy celebrating Christmas at my parents' house, but this feels completely off the charts.

We finish our mugs of goodness and Brian leads us back into the house where a fire is blazing in the living room. A Christmas tree stands off to the side of the fireplace, gracing a large back window. I meander towards it when the outdoor lights turn on as darkness scoots across the landscape. I gasp as I see a family of deer dart directly behind the house, kicking up snow as they pass.

"Did you see that, Mommy?" Mattie points to the hollowed out prints in the snow as if I needed evidence.

"I did, Mattie. That was a wonderful treat."

"At first I thought they were Brian's reindeer, but they looked different," Mattie says.

"Oh yes, we get all sorts of wildlife out here. I think they are attracted to the place because of all the animals I have." He winks at Mattie and adds, "Of course it could be for the easy food they can get visiting the barns." Mattie giggles and leaves to find Ethan.

I look up to see Brian looking at me with a lopsided grin. As handsome as he is in his jeans and cowboy hat, this look fits him as well. My heart races as his head drops closer. *Oh-em-gee, is he going to kiss me right here in front of all his family?* He whispers softly, “Thank you for coming tonight and letting us have a fresh start.”

Like a fool, I just nod. The truth be known, he’s paralyzed my throat with his nearness. My mouth has forgotten how to speak. Being his typical self, he returns my grin and wraps an arm through mine. I float alongside of him as he stops to refill our mugs.

“I really shouldn’t have another. It’s dark and snowing. I have to navigate the road home later.”

He peers back outside where the flurries have picked up and is piling snow against the windowsill. “Just in case, Rita had the foresight to make up a room for you and the kids to stay over.” He shrugs his shoulders and says, “It’s a habit at Christmas. We enjoy ourselves and have ‘sleep-overs’ so none of us have to worry about if all will get homes safely. I hope you’ll stay.”

I reach out brushing his fingers as I take the mug of wine and smile. “How can I resist?”

“I was hoping you would see it that way.”

I’m practically oblivious to the chatter and noise surrounding us. I’m held in his eyes and feel like I’m falling from cloud to cloud, suspended in a heaven of delight. Soon enough, Brian breaks eye contact and I hear Connie and Rita fussing whether the pies are done enough and where to set out all the food.

“Is there anything I can do to help?” I move into the kitchen and inhale all the wondrous aromas coming off the food.

“Yes. You can make sure you brought a hefty appetite! I think we over did it again,” Rita chimes.

Brian nudged her, then hugged her shoulders. “Rita is bad enough on her own but when Mom comes, it’s like dueling chefs.”

Connie laughs. “Yes, but I never hear you complaining as you pile your plate full.”

He pretends to take offense, then laughs deeply. "The day I complain about being given such wonderful cooking is the day I should be locked away. You'll never get a complaint from me."

I'm enjoying their banter and it makes me wonder what it would have been like with a brother or sister growing up and then returning home for the holidays together. They truly love each other's company and I feel so grateful that Mattie and Ethan are here to see this. I hope it becomes a lifelong memory.

They finally decide to make the dinner a buffet-style and line all the food on the center bar. Rita shuffles over to the dinner table and collects the China plates, placing them at one end of the buffet. "Here, George and I will help the children with their plates, the rest of you load up your own!"

I try to let them know it's no trouble, I'm used to getting their plates, but they won't hear of it and swoosh me aside as they have the children point to what they want. I wait for Rita to pick up a plate and then I move behind her. I should have let Brian step in front of me because now I'm conscious of his closeness behind me. I feel the heat coming off his body—okay, it may be the mulled wine and I grin to myself. They have outdone themselves with this meal. I gnaw on my lip trying to choose what to add to my plate. There is turkey with dressing, pineapple topped ham, mashed potatoes, giblet gravy, cranberry sauce, yams with marshmallows melting down their sides, asparagus with lemon wedges, green bean salad, creamed corn, and a large salad with every vegetable under the sun piled in there.

Brian asks, "Dark meat or light?" He has his tongs hovering over the turkey.

"Dark, please."

He takes a portion and drops it on my plate as he reaches next to it and adds a slice of ham, smiling. He whispers, "You have to have both. Mom made the turkey and Rita made the ham." I grin at his ploy to keep the cooks happy.

I add a small helping of all but the salad to my plate, and it's about to run over. I find a place next to Mattie and Ethan and take a seat. They're being extra good and sit with their hands folded in their laps, waiting for everyone else to sit down. Rita and Connie sit on the other side of the table and Brian sits at the end, next to me, as George takes the other end next to his wife.

Mattie pipes up. "May I say grace?"

I see Connie's eyes glisten as she moves her napkin close to her heart. "That would be delightful."

We bow our heads and listen to Mattie's prayer. I'm near tears as she ends the prayer thanking God and all at the table for this special day. I can't be prouder of her.

Instead of quiet and decorum, the jokes abound. Rita starts with, "Why does Scrooge like Santa's reindeer so much? Because every buck is *deer* to him!"

I snort laugh and that starts a chain reaction of giggles. Brian nudges me and says, "What do you call an obnoxious deer? Rude-olf!" Tears are running down my cheeks at these bad jokes, but it's so funny to hear them from adults who are all laughing and enjoying their time together.

"My turn!" Connie stands and says, "What does Santa tell his reindeer before telling them a joke? This one is going to sleigh you!" We all laugh and I'm to the point of holding my sides, it hurts to laugh so much.

Of course, the mulled wine helps considerably, but I no longer care. I'm on cloud nine, I'm having so much fun. I look around the table as I scoop up some of the mashed potatoes and gravy. I don't want to hear another joke when I take a bite. During this pause, I see everyone else is having the same thought and the laughter starts all over again.

George tries to take control and stands at the far end of the table, clanging his knife against his mug. "Mother, kids, get a hold of yourselves. I want to do more than stare at this delicious dinner. I've had to smell the aroma all day long, and my stomach is dying to have it in my belly."

I bite the inside of my lip, trying desperately to not laugh. Connie blinks back her tears of laughter. She looks at George and says quite calmly, "If Rudolf had a wife, he would say…yes *deer*."

That's it… we all drop our utensils onto our plates and belly laugh until it hurts. To make it worse, Brian has the nose runs and the laughing is making it bubble and we all roar with laugher and point. All of us -- except the kids, who are mystified why the grown-ups have lost it -- hurry away from the table and try to get under control. Without coats, hats, or gloves, we rush out to the porch, allowing the freezing wind to suck the laughter out of us. Within a few minutes, we are able to return to the house and to the table. With the spent energy from all the laughing, the food looks twice as tasty and the sounds around the table are of the delicious food disappearing.

CHAPTER 17

I find myself thanking my lucky stars for having that flat tire and my wonderful neighbor for calling Brian to come fix it for me. I can't believe how a thing like a flat tire has me enjoying such wonderful company and the best day ever.

I help clear the table and pass on dessert. I'm not the only one that can't fit another bite in at the moment. We move to the living room and Rita brings out some old games for Mattie and Ethan to play with as we lounge in front of the crackling fireplace. I sit on the couch with Rita and her mom, while Brian sits in a very large leather recliner.

"So what says all—should we all bundle up and take a sleigh ride?" Brian wiggles his eyebrows as he asks.

Connie says, "It wouldn't feel like Christmas if we didn't!"

"I thought you would say so. I have the top on the wagon and the hay and blankets ready. All I have to do is hitch the tractor."

"Son, I'll help you hitch it up." George stands and slips on his jacket and disappears out the door with Brian.

Ethan brings me his jacket, scarf, and has his rainbow-colored gloves ready to wiggle into. Mattie puts on her new cape, which, being made of wool, should keep her warm enough with us sitting beneath the snuggly blankets. I sigh, wishing for once Brian could ride with us and not be the puller.

"I've got a batch of hot cocoa ready for us when we return. The ride is too bumpy to carry it along with us," Rita says.

Hearing the bells jingling on the hay wagon, Ethan bounces in front of me as I try to switch his cowboy hat to a warm, knitted cap. "Mommy, this hat is extra warm, just like all the real cowboys wear. Don't you remember the TV shows? They never wore knitted caps."

I have to grin. He has a valid argument and being with company, I allow him the cowboy hat. I glance to see Connie with her hands clasped together. I can read her eyes. She simply adores being around children. It finally dawns on me... they have no grandchildren. That's why the generosity. I bet the last time they had a child around was when Samantha and her son stayed with Brian. I also wonder what they thought of Samantha and whether Samantha hid her true colors around them. Well, that is two minutes I'll never get back, thinking of that she-devil.

Outside, the snow comes down heavily, but it's so beautiful the way it mounds over everything. The lights turn everything into blurry runs of color reflected off the mounds.

Brian removes the safety rail and helps us all into the wagon, jumping in behind us and slipping the safety rail back into place. He rubs his hands together and plops down right next to me, pulling a blanket over our laps.

"Dad wants to drive us tonight. I guess we'll trust him on that, since he's the only one that didn't drink our mulled wine!" I giggle and feel like I'm having a heat flash—at my age!

Rita leads us into "Rudolf the Red-Nosed Reindeer" and we all join in. The kids beam. I'm still in disbelief of how wonderful life is in this moment. It could have all been lost had Brian not sent the Christmas card, the one explaining what Samantha had been up to. I really can't blame her as much as I want to, because here I am, enjoying Brian and his family and seeing a future where we'll be included in these magical moments.

I jump in my seat. I've been too busy in reflection to notice Brian has moved his hand under the blanket and reached for mine. He almost pulls his hand away thinking I'm upset, rather than startled. I quickly wrap my fingers into his, locking him in place. When I look into his eyes, a smile is reflected there. Suddenly, I feel like we are all alone, everything has faded away. My heart quickens and I hope for this ride to last all night.

George hits a snowbank and we are all thrown from side to side. Connie shrieks, but hangs on tightly to the railing and doesn't fall. He stops the tractor and Brian jumps over the side to see what we're dealing with.

"Well gang, I think we should bring this ride to a halt and head back to the house. The snow has blown so much, it's covered the trail and we'll soon get stuck if we continue. It's too easy to get off the trail and into the ditch."

"That's fine, son. It's colder out here than I thought it would be, and that hot cocoa sounds really delicious right now." Connie rubs her mittens together, attempting to get warmth down to her fingers.

I nod and the kids, of course, are just fine with the possibility of hot cocoa and more sweets. I will only miss sitting here with Brian so close and holding my hand. George brings us to a slow turn and we head back towards the house. It's colder now with the wind in our face, and the snow blows directly into the wagon. It's a smart call to go back to the cabin. George stops the tractor by the porch as Brian helps us all out of the wagon. After a moment or two of discussion, Brian convinces his dad to climb down and go warm up inside. He'll take the wagon to the barn.

While the others line up in the kitchen to get their hot cocoa, I stand nervously by the door and stare out into the shifting snow. The minutes seem like hours. I'm afraid he'll be frozen stiff out there. If it was so easy to get the wagon off course, it would be just as easy for Brian to get lost in the blinding snow. Did he even have a flashlight? I nibble on my gloves as I watch. Beyond the porch, it's too dark to see. My racing heart threatens to leap from my chest. Wait, I think I see...yes! It's a bobbing light headed towards the porch.

He stomps on the porch, dislodging a mountain of packed snow off his shoes and legs. He sees me standing there waiting.

A smile spreads across his face and mine must match how his looks. He comes in and without thought, I hurry to him and hug him close. Once I realize what I just did, I try to step back, but he holds me tight for a moment longer. A most wonderful, beautiful, moment longer. He pulls away, but only by inches, pointing above us and leaning in for a kiss. I become lost in his warmth. His kiss shoots through me with an electrical charge. We break apart aware that the room had gone silent. My cheeks turn crimson as I turn to see all the grinning faces staring at us. Brian breaks the stares by saying, "Mistletoe." Fortunately, Mattie and Ethan are too busy shoveling up sweets to have caught us under the mistletoe. I nibble on my lower lip, thinking it's much too early for them to see their Mommy kissing another man. We walk together towards the hot cocoa as Rita uncovers the bounty of desserts, urging us to eat our fill. The only thing I'm hungry for is more of those kisses…

My phone pings in my pocket and I hurry to shut it off. My shoulders deflate. It's Greg. "Hello?"

"Hey, Darci, let me talk to the kids."

"It's a little late to be calling them. Maybe tomorrow would be better."

"Tomorrow isn't Christmas. Let me talk to them."

I can hear a slight slur to his words, and I know how he gets when he's had a few. Being in front of guests, I don't want this call to become the focal point. "Let me round them up. Hang on." I mute the call and ask Brian if there is somewhere I can take the kids to let them talk to their father. He nods and shows me to the den. I call them over to me and close the door.

"Mattie, it's your Daddy. He wants to wish you a Merry Christmas." I put the phone on speaker so I can make sure he doesn't say anything to ruin their day.

"Goody!" Taking the phone, she says, "Merry Christmas, Daddy!"

"Hi, pumpkin! How is your Christmas? I'm sorry your gift hasn't arrived yet, it's been so crazy at work. I think I'll tell

Mommy where it is and she can run by and get it for you and Ethan. How's that? I wouldn't want my pumpkin to miss out on presents."

"Oh, you don't have to worry Daddy, we got lots of presents already. And guess what?"

"What?"

"Ethan and I both got ponies for Christmas!"

"Are they stick ponies?

"No, Daddy," she giggles. "They're real!"

"Who got you ponies? Aren't you still living at your Granny's house?"

"Oh no, Daddy. We have a nice apartment."

"I don't think you can keep a pony in an apartment."

Mattie laughs as if she was told the funniest joke in the world. I, on the other hand, feel my face heating up. No doubt he is going to make a big issue out of this since his children are happy and someone else gave them a gift.

"You're funny, Daddy. No, the ponies stay here at Brian's place. He has lots of space for them and we can come over anytime we want to feed and ride them. He also has reindeer, Daddy. Reindeer!"

"Listen, Mattie, I need to talk you your Mommy, okay? Love ya and Merry Christmas."

"I love you too, Daddy. Bye."

She hands me the phone and I take it off the speaker. "Don't make a big deal with this, Greg."

"Who is this Brian and why is he giving my kids such extravagant gifts? Are you at his house now? Listen, Darci, I don't want strange men around my children. There is no telling why he's given them ponies. You hear all sorts of strange things in the world."

"I know who he is, and better than that, I know his whole family. I'm not having this discussion with you today. Do you want to talk to Ethan?" I hear him guzzling down another drink.

"Hell, I guess I better before he forgets who his real Daddy is."

"Don't talk like that and I want you to know, you'll be on the speaker so be nice."

I call Ethan to me and he's bopping up and down. "Hi, Daddy!"

"Hi, Peanut. I hear you have a new pony."

"Yes and he's beautiful…"

"You be real careful riding him, horses can be dangerous."

"Not him, he's special. He's used to giving kids rides. I'll have Mommy get you a picture like she gave me. It shows me really good on the pony."

"I'd like that, Peanut. Listen, I told Mattie my presents haven't gotten there yet…"

"Don't worry, Daddy. This Christmas was the best Christmas ever! I have me a new cowboy leather jacket and cowboy hat and games and pictures and…"

"That's nice. Merry Christmas, son. I need to talk to your Mommy."

"Okay, Daddy. Bye." Ethan gives me the phone and asks if they can go finish their desserts. I nod and open the door for them.

"I have to go, Greg. Thanks for wishing them a Merry Christmas."

"Yeah, whatever. Just know this isn't finished. I want to know who is messing around my kids. You hear me?"

I hang up and turn down the volume on the phone. My stomach is in knots. It never did take much for Greg to get under my skin and ruin a day. Well, not this time, buddy. I slip the phone back into my pocket, take a deep breath, and join the others in the kitchen. I thought every eye would be on me when I entered, but I'm wrong. They are laughing and eating as if nothing even happened. I let out a breath I didn't know I'd been holding.

Chapter 18

Brian gravitates towards me, giving a concerned smile. "Is everything okay?"

"Sure is, now I think I want some of that apple pie."

Rita throws her hands on her hips. "Apple pie? That's so everyday. Why not have a slice of my very *special* pecan pie?"

Connie mocks a hurt look and fakes a pout on her face.

"You know, I think I'll have a slice of both pies." Laughter spills around the bar as they both go to town cutting their pies.

Brian leans over and whispers, "That's the only way to keep them happy." Then, he winks.

Flutters stir in my stomach, like a swarm of butterflies shooting up in the sky all at once. How can he do something as simple as a wink and I get all giddy? I grin at him when I see his mom slide a plate over to him, followed by Rita sending him a plate of pecan pie topped to the sky with whipped cream. We pull up a stool on the corner of the bar and dive into the deliciousness. I wish I would have put on those stretch pants, as the top button now feels like it will pop at any moment. It's a very good thing I love pies. "Mmm," I mumble through a full mouth to the happy smiles of Brian's family. I do think I've landed in a piece of heaven here at Brian's. It's amazing to me that I have only known him for a short while and only just recently met his parents, but it feels like I've known them most of my life. How can I get so lucky?

Rita suddenly stiffens as she checks her phone. I see the color drain from her face and I know without anyone saying a thing, it's Samantha. What is it, radar? The most miserable people want to drag everyone else down? Rita pulls Brian to the side and shows him the text. His face goes from jubilant to mad in two seconds flat.

He turns to look at me, scratching his head before looking to his mom. Her forehead bunches up with concern. He pulls me over to the door by the porch and holds me tight, his chin nestled on the top of my head, then steps back. "I didn't think anything could make this day go bad. I apologize in advance. I bet you guessed who texted Rita…"

"Yes. To see everyone's face crumble, it was obvious."

"She's in town to celebrate Christmas with her family. She *says* she wanted to drop off presents to Rita and me. She says she stopped by Rita's and no one was home so she'll just drive over and drop off the presents. Rita tried to text her back, but she isn't answering."

My chest caves in. Not so much for Brian, because I know he can handle whatever she throws his way, but for her son, Billy. It hurts my heart that she could use him yet again to wiggle back into Brian's life. "What about Billy?"

"I can't make any promises, but she said she just ran out saying she had to run errands and left Billy at her parents' place. I'm going to sit at the gate and tell her she's not welcome." Please, Darci, do not leave. Don't let her take our wonderful day."

"No, I won't go home, Brian, but if you don't mind, I'd like to go with you. Maybe if she knows someone else… cares for you, she'll know she is wasting time."

"You would do that? Wait with me for Samantha?" He looks utterly shocked.

"I almost have to. That is, if it won't bother you. It's just that I don't want her to plant any more seeds of deception like she's done before."

He bends in and kisses the top of my head. “Listen all, we are going to the gate to take care of something. It won’t take long. I expect to hear laughing and singing when we get back!” I glance around this wonderful family and already think the world of them. Connie’s eyes are glistening with unshed tears. She must be very proud of her son. He’s been a stand-up guy since I’ve met him and no one will convince me otherwise.

We bundle up and jump in his truck. The snow is thick, but he has four-wheel drive and makes it over the mounding snow with no problem. I can’t imagine why Samantha would get out in weather like this. In town they would have the trucks out sanding the roads, but not once you pull off of the main thoroughfares. I’m shivering up a storm and Brian wraps an arm around me, pulling me in close to him. I’m in paradise. His cologne is a warm, woodsy scent of cedar mixed with musk and definitely is working its magic on me. The heater finally knocks the ice off my toes by the time we reach the gate. Leaning forward, Brian turns off the truck lights and we sit in the darkness, waiting.

I slip forward out of his arm, shrugging off my coat. “Your heater sure kicks the warmth in gear.” I scoot off to the side a bit, trying to be nonchalant. The truth is, here in the darkness and so close to him that I can feel his pulse, my heartrate is through the roof.

He turns sideways, smiling. “Don’t worry. This will be over with soon and she won’t interfere with us again. I guess we all have a bit of the past to contend with, but it doesn’t need to impact our future. All I know is, I want you in my future, Darci. When I’m around you it’s like I’ve stepped out of a black and white movie and into full color.”

“I enjoy your company and I know there is chemistry between us, but I need to go slow.” I know my heart wants to leap out of my chest as much as I want to fall into his strong arms, but I have to be cautious for my children. “The kids adore you and…well, it’s been such a short time, I don’t want to make any mistakes that would cause them anymore sadness.”

He raises my hand to his lips and kisses it, then covers it with his other hand, holding it tight. "We'll go as slow as you're comfortable with. Oh, I almost forgot..." Dropping my hand, he reaches into his coat pocket and pulls out a small, gift-wrapped package. "Merry Christmas!"

My eyes spring wide-open as I grin. "Now, when did you have time today to run out shopping?"

"Honestly, I picked this up at the Christmas Extravaganza... before everything hit a sour note. It reminded me of you—of us, and what brought us together."

I look at him puzzled. "A flat tire?"

His laughter rocks the truck. Shaking his head no, he motions for me to unwrap it.

In spite of the heat, goosebumps travel up my arms to my neck. I can't believe he found a gift for me weeks ago at the event, at the very time I thought he and Samantha were back together. After peeling the paper away, I see a small jewelry box and my mouth goes dry. Tentatively, I ease the lid open. Surprise catches the edges of my lips as I grin and tears form in my eyes. "Brian, it's beautiful and a perfect reminder of our first Christmas." I bite my lip after saying our first Christmas, afraid I've over-stepped. I clumsily try to remove the necklace from the box, but my fingers won't cooperate.

He reaches over and frees the necklace, having me turn so he can place it around my neck and clasp it. I lift it up and look at it. A perfect silver reindeer with a little red bow-styled scarf around its tiny neck. "I love it! Thank you so much. It's beautiful and absolutely perfect." As I look up into his eyes, he leans forward, placing a hand on my cheek, and kisses me. His kiss deepens as he draws me in closer. I'm lost in his embrace, in his touch. I melt into him, returning the passion of his kiss. Suddenly, bright lights flare into the truck.

We pull apart and he says, "Stay warm. This won't take long." Swinging the door open, he slides from the truck and crunches through the snow to stand by the gate. Punching the gate code in, he allows it to slide open enough for him to pass through. When Samantha sees him head towards her car, she springs out of it wearing a Santa's hat and a deep plunging sweater with skintight black leggings. Her arms wrap around his neck, pulling him towards a kiss. My mouth goes dry. I can't believe she is up to the same old tricks.

Brian becomes animated, pushing her arms away and backing away from her. I see him pointing behind her. He must be telling her to leave. I glide the window down a smidge, listening.

"I told you we were over. How many times do I have to tell you? I don't want to hear from you and I certainly don't want to see you. I mean it, Samantha. The only decent thing you've done tonight is not dragging Billy along with you. How could you even leave him on Christmas to go driving around looking for what? A booty call?" He shakes his head, filled with frustration.

"What, do you have the snooty bimbo with you *this* Christmas? She can't offer you what I can."

I feel my blood boiling. I want to run out there and dash her head in the snow and commence filling her mouth with it until she shuts her trap.

"The only bimbo around here is you. Go home, Samantha. You aren't welcome around here. Ever. I won't have you trying to wreck my life again. Just—leave!" He spins on his boots and slides through the gate, locking it back in place.

She starts screaming at the top of her lungs and throws her car door open and flings presents over the gate. One hits him square in his back. He keeps walking away from her and climbs back into the truck, his face flushed with anger. "I'm so sorry you had to see that." He shifts the truck into reverse and we back away from the gate. Doing a three-point maneuver, he turns us towards his cabin.

Behind us, Samantha climbs into her car, slams it into reverse and spins out into the roadway, her horn blaring down the road. I'm at a loss for words. She has certainly dampened the evening. We both sit silently as he drives us slowly through the thickly, blanketed road. When we come to the bend in the road, he slips the truck into park and leans against the steering wheel, cradling it with his arms, his head tucked inside. I slide over to him, rubbing his back, hating that he had been put through such a scene. He falls back against the seat. "How can I still let her get to me this way? Just to see her makes me angry. She sucks the life out of everything she touches. I got to hand it to her, if it was on her list to ruin Christmas, she succeeded."

"Only if you let her. What's fifteen minutes out of our day?" I smile gently and turn his face to me. "Let's not let her take up any more of our time, okay?"

He pulls me into a hug. We sit there with the snow gently falling, surrounded by the wash of Christmas lights reflected across the snow. We hold onto each other and let the peace of the ranch wrap us in its warmth.

"I'm ready for that hot chocolate that's waiting for us inside. How about you?"

He smiles and nods and slips the truck into drive. "I think with a shot of something a bit stronger."

I grin and say, "A little Fireball might hit the spot…"

He looks at me in surprise and slams his hands against the steering wheel. "You're *on,* little lady!"

CHAPTER 19

I concentrate on remembering how wonderful the day has been, up to the moment the text message arrived. I'm determined not to allow these past few minutes destroy our Christmas. My fingers find his arm where he's pushed up his sweater and jacket sleeves in frustration. I'm drawn to his arm, the way his hair fills around the muscles. I sigh. I've always been attracted to the look of a man's forearm, the strength in it, the look of protection it offers. I rub my hand over his forearm and slip in close to him again. I'm tired of fighting what I feel with him, and I'm not about to let the last fifteen minutes with Samantha steal away our day. By the time we reach the front door, we both feel much better.

Brian opens the front door and I expect to see a solemn look across everyone's faces, but instead, Connie and George are sitting on the floor with Mattie and Ethan playing a game while Rita is lining up the hot cocoa mugs and filling them. She turns and raises an eyebrow to Brian, to which he responds by giving her a huge hug. He then slips behind her to reach into the corner liquor cabinet, pulling out a pint of that fiery drink. I rarely sample it, but tonight is made for something just like it. Brian quickly pours two shot glasses full and hands one to me.

"To hellos and goodbyes." Brian smiles as he clinks his glass to mine.

"Let's leave it as just to 'hellos,'" I say. "Or, "Here's to more of *our* hellos."

"I like that even better. I'll make a deal with you," he says pulling out his phone, "I'll turn off my phone if you do the same. That way, we don't risk being bothered again this wonderful night."

I smile. "Deal."

"Well, I'll pass on that liquid fire but I'll turn mine off as well. After all, the people I care most about are all together in this house." Rita slips her phone out of her jeans and shuts it down.

It feels like there is, finally, Peace on Earth.

Slowly, the fire dies down in the fireplace and the children's sugar rush turns into yawns. I ask Rita to show us where we'll be sleeping so I can get them to bed before they nod away. We are on the second story about mid-hallway. There is a bathroom between where we will sleep and Rita's room. She points further down the hall to show where their parents' room is located and just around the bend in the hallway, all the way back, is where Brian has his room. We return downstairs not a minute too soon. Ethan has his head on Mattie's shoulder, his cowboy hat all askew. Brian comes over and lifts him to his shoulder as I get Mattie to stumble toward the staircase.

As we get to our room, Brian gently lays the little cowboy down on a well-prepared cot and pulls a thick quilt up to his chin, carefully slipping the cowboy hat off and placing it under the cot. I slip Mattie into the bed she and I will share. I'm able to quickly remove her Christmas cloak and her boots and scoot her to the far side of the bed. I stand and turn to see Brian smiling sweetly at us. If there was ever a man born to be a father, I have to say it's Brian. He loves everything there is about children and that is a rare commodity. He leans in and gives me a tender kiss. Not too long and not too short, one that holds promises for tomorrows as well as the understanding that we will take as long as necessary to build our relationship to survive any storm.

Crawling into the plush bed, I sink into a cloud of happiness. Even with Greg's call and Samantha showing up, this day has been the very best day I can remember. I snuggle deep into the blankets, my eyes twinkling as much as any Christmas lights could. I relive the day moment by moment from the time I read the Christmas card from Brian. I want to shake my head. That part of it seems like it was days ago! Closing my eyes, I let the day replay under my closed lids until sleep can take me away.

Sometime during the night or early morning, I hear someone rustling about. I roll gently off the mattress, ready to head to the door when Ethan wakes up with a start.

"Mommy! Where are we?" He has that high-pitched worry in his words, which means in a few seconds he will go into a full pitched cry.

"Shhh, honey. Remember, we went to Brian's last night. We all stayed up late and they made us this wonderful guest room to stay in so we didn't have to drive home in the snow."

"My hat! I can't find my new hat," he says with a tremble in his words.

"Here it is. Under your cot so it won't get smashed. See? There is nothing to be worried about."

"Will you sit by me for a while?"

"Of course. Now, close your eyes and remember all the wonderful parts of your Christmas day. I'll sing "Silent Night" if you'll keep your eyes closed and a smile on your lips."

"Okay, but can you rub my hair while you sing?"

"I wouldn't have it any other way."

Ethan snuggles deep into his cot with the quilt pulled up under his chin. I sit on the floor at the front edge of the cot and stroke his hair as I begin singing in a quiet tone. I don't think I made it to the chorus before he is sound asleep. Standing, I listen to the house and it all seems quiet, so I slip back under the covers and fall back to sleep.

When I awake, there is no mistaking it this time. It sounds as if everyone is up. The voices fade as they leave the hallway and head downstairs. Opening the door, I see the hallway lights are on and the bathroom door is ajar. I hurry to the restroom, and while in there I hear Rita talking to her mom.

"I had to tell him, mom. There was no way around it."

"I just don't understand that woman. Having the nerve to drive out here last night and start things with Brian. She should have stayed home." Connie huffed.

"That doesn't matter now. We all have to understand that Brian is going to need all of our support."

I know my eyes must be as big as a saucer. When I open the bathroom door, I walk to Rita's room and lightly knock. The room grows quiet and then I hear movement.

"Rita, are you alright? I thought I had heard people going up and down the stairs."

"I'm sorry, Darci. We had some early morning news that caught us off guard. I'm sorry we woke you. Are the children still sleeping?" Connie says. Her face shows worry and I think that is so sweet of her to worry thinking they've woken the children.

"Oh no, they are still sleeping."

Connie looks to Rita and then back to me. Rita nods.

"I'll sit with the children while you and Rita go get some coffee. They'll be fine. If they wake while you're gone, I'll bring them downstairs for something to eat." She says all this with a warm smile.

"I accept. Coffee sounds great."

Rita hooks her arm through mine and we slip out of her room with Connie following us long enough to open the bedroom door, smile at the sleeping children, and sit in the rocker next to the window.

I'm surprised not to see Brian as we reach the bottom of the stairs. I imagine he is already at it in the barns tending to the animals. Judging by the amount of coffee left in the pot, he should be bright-eyed and bushy-tailed, as mom would say. I sit at one end of the couch and Rita sits next to me. This is the first time I've taken notice of her face. She looks—strained.

"Is everything okay? Has something happened?"

"Darci, it's terrible. There is no way to say it except to come out and say it. Samantha had an accident last night after she left here."

I gasp. My hand is shaking, rattling the spoon in my cup. "Is she okay?" I flash back to last evening and even with everything she did and how she did it, this was the last thing I expected to hear. I physically ache for her and her son.

"No, dear. She's in and out of it due to the pain. The—the worse thing is Billy. He had tried calling all night, but we had our phones turned off. He was near hysterics when he reached Brian this morning."

My throat has turned to sand. Billy. I feel the hot tears burning down my cheek.

"Mom is irritated with me because I turned by phone on first and had a text message from him. I showed it to Brian."

I look up at her and see the pain she carries in her eyes. I feel in my gut things are about to turn worse.

"I was next to him when he called Billy…" She pauses, wipes her nose dry, and looks at me with tears in her eyes. "Billy is so lost with his mother in the hospital. He begged Brian to come get him. Brian said he would first go see Samantha in the hospital. Darci… he blames himself for the accident."

"But… it wasn't his fault! You should have seen the way she tore out from the gate to the road."

"I know, I know. This is simply the way Brian is. He takes responsibility even when it's not his to take. Mom is livid. She knows what kind of person Samantha is and was ecstatic to meet you and the kids. Now she feels Samantha will worm her way back into Brian's life.

"Did you say he's bringing Billy here? To stay until his mom is released from the hospital?"

"I don't know if it was shock talking when he said it, but he certainly feels guilty enough to do so. He doesn't think Samantha's mom will give Billy the kind of attention he will need right now, this is her only daughter and she's really upset. Then there is her work schedule and Billy being on school holiday… it's all a bit much for her."

My stomach drops. I do understand his concern for the boy and what Samantha is going through, but memories start circling my brain. The way he calls Brian "Poppa Brian." The way he feels this ranch is his since Brian started buying all the animals while Billy lived there. Rita reaches over and grasps my hand.

"Try to understand the hurt Brian feels. Don't let it tear you both in two."

"I don't know what to think at the moment, Rita. It's all a shock. I think it's time for me to get the kids ready to go home. You understand, don't you? I don't think it would be—good for us to be here if he brings Billy here. Tell Brian he can call or stop by later if he feels like it, okay?"

She nods and rises with me to go back upstairs. Mattie is already awake and sitting in Connie's lap, reading her a book. The picture is priceless. The look of genuine love pouring out of Connie as Mattie reads causes my chin to tremble.

"Mattie, honey, we need to get ready to go home. Will you wake Ethan and help him with his shoes while I get the car heated up and ready?"

"Sure, Mommy. Can we come back later?"

"We'll see. Brian had an emergency come up, so we'll have to wait until things get… better."

"Is he okay, Mommy?"

"Oh yes, sugar. He is fine. Now hurry along. Connie will stay here with your while I get the car ready, okay?"

"Okay, Mommy."

As I walk downstairs it feels like all the walls are crumbling around me. I have to get the children home before they see me cry. I tell myself this is just a bump in the road, but my intuition tells me differently. Brian won't walk away from this. That isn't the kind of man he is. The longer Samantha is in the hospital—well, I'm not going to get in the middle of it all.

Scraping the snow off the windshield with a vengeance, I have the car purring like a kitten in no time. As I walk back into the house, Ethan and Mattie are coming down the stairs with Connie holding their hands. It isn't hard to tell she is fighting her own tears back.

"It was a beautiful evening we shared with you, Connie. I can't thank you enough for the children's presents."

"We haven't had such a wonderful time in eons. We are thrilled to have met you and hope… we will see each other again soon." I catch the pause in her throat after she said hope. Yes, hope is what we will keep buried in our hearts.

Connie gives them candy cane cookies for their journey home. How could I say no?

Driving up to the gate, I see the thrown packages from last night have been picked up and the gate left open. Seeing it this way makes me feel as if we are the ones that shouldn't be here. As afraid as I am to hear from Brian, I don't think I'll rest until I do.

Once home, Mattie and Ethan rush to their toys and begin playing while I excuse myself to my room. I lie on the bed, staring at the ceiling. Already the memories of last night start to fade with the shock of the new day.

CHAPTER 20

Just as I turn over on the bed, my phone rings. It's enough to make my heart start racing. Fumbling in my purse, I snatch it up and answer.

"Hi, sweetie. Your dad wanted me to check on what time we all wanted to leave to see Mattie and Ethan's new ponies." The gaiety in her voice catches me off-guard. Mom.

"Hi, mom."

"I didn't wake you, did I? You sound…"

"Oh, no, mom. It's just, well, we aren't going to be able to go to Brian's today. A friend was in an accident last night and well, things are a bit hectic over there right now."

"I'm so sorry to hear that. Say, was it that woman on the news late last night? The one that crashed and flipped her car?"

"It might be. I didn't watch the news last night."

"It was just terrible, crashing like that on Christmas evening! Well, any time, really. That's partially why I called so early. We were worried for you. All that snow last night and you and the children were probably there very late." Her sigh goes straight to my eardrum. "At any rate, I truly hope her family is near and can be with her. Please let me know her update when Brian calls you, will you?"

"Um, sure, mom. No problem. Let dad know we are safe and sound. We'll have a lazy day around here. I'm sure all of us could stand a few long naps today."

"I hear that and I didn't have to eat two full Christmas meals, either!"

Ugh. Will she ever let me live it down? Besides, a lot of families have double meals to eat when you have in-laws and the like.

"So funny, mom. But, yes, I'm sure all the extra calories are part of what is making us so sleepy today. We'll catch up soon. I promise."

"Don't forget to call me when you learn more about that poor woman."

"I won't, mom. Hugs to you and dad. Talk to you later."

I disconnect before she can add more salt to the wound. Bless her. She has no idea what an impact this is making for me and the kids. I dread explaining it to them, but sure as I don't, they'll find out from someone else. I'm getting many déjà vu from my life. I don't know how my mom did it, but practically anything that happened at school, mom knew it way before I could tell her. This would be no different. I just hope when Brian calls, I'll have some better news to stir into the conversation.

Checking on the children, I see Ethan almost asleep, his arm dangling off the couch with his toy car clutched tight in his fist. Mattie's head is bobbing, trying to stay upright watching cartoons. I scoop her up first and take her to their room to slip her into some pajamas. By the time I'm finished, she's ready to snuggle into her own bed and dream of their best Christmas ever. I sniffle looking at her. How can things take a turn for the worst in a few short hours?

Ethan is asleep. His car now out of his tiny fist and resting on the carpet below him. Once I have him in my arms, I grab up his cowboy hat and take them both to the room. I make sure to place his hat on his nightstand so he'll be sure to see it when he awakens. Now in his pajamas, I slip him deep under his covers and return to my room. As much as I want to jump in the shower, the bed looks too inviting and I'm sure I won't hear anything from Brian until later in the day. Crawling out of my Christmas clothes, I get my warm jammies on and pull back the covers on my bed. I'll take advantage of this quiet time and catch a few winks while I can. I have no idea of what comes next, but Brian may need us there later, after he returns from the hospital and seeing Billy. I'm going to need all the rest I can get by then.

I awaken and it's almost eleven o'clock. I must have been tired. I peek into the children's room and they are still snoozing up a storm. Perfect time to hit the shower and let all that warm water ease the tension in my muscles. I let the water heat up until steam is heavy on the mirror and slip inside the shower, immediately glad for the relaxing thrumming of the showerhead pulsating as I roll my shoulders, letting the heat massage those muscles before plunging my head underneath the falling cascade of water. I stand there until the water starts to cool down. Rarely do I indulge in such an over-use of water, but this one time it feels more like therapy than a simple shower. I look at the pile in the floor of my comfy-cozy jammies. As much as I want to stay in them all day, there is no telling if Brian will stop by on his way home, so I opt for a baggy sweater and warm sweatpants that have the word *Fearless* printed all over them. Boy, how I wish that were true. I shrug my shoulders and hope they instill more fearlessness into me just by the wearing.

Towel-drying my hair, I slip it into a scrunchie and brush my teeth, hoping to remove at least half the calories I ate yesterday. If only! Grabbing the book from my nightstand, I wiggle under the covers with my pillows propping my head up. I look down to see a flashing light on my phone. A missed call. Oh no. I missed a call from Brian!

Punching in his number, I ring him back.

"Hello?" Brian answers.

Just as the smile floods my face, I hear background noise.

"Is that my mom? Will she get to come home today?"

Billy. Billy is with Brian. And from the sound of it, they are at the cabin.

"Hi, Brian. I missed your call while in the shower." I roll my eyes, not even sure why I needed to let him know I had been in the shower. *Get a grip, Darci.*

"Hi, Darci. Could you hang on for a second?"

"Of course."

I hear some muted talking taking place and then a door closes. Ah, he must be in the study.

"Sorry about that, Darci. Uh, anyway, I wanted to let you know what I found out."

"Thank you, Brian. I've been worried once I heard—about the accident. Is Billy there at the cabin with you?"

He pauses a few seconds longer than I expected.

"Brian? Everything okay?"

"Yes and no, Darci. It's a mess. And complicated."

I catch my breath. I'm sure the world is starting to crumble around me. I can't seem to say a word. Brian, hearing my long pause, fills the gap. I listen, blinking away tears.

"Darci? Are you still there?"

"Yes, Brian. I wish I could say I didn't understand why Billy and Samantha will be living with you, but you already explained that she will need help while she's in her casts, something that I gather her *mom* can't provide."

"She can't, Darci, she'll be at work a great deal of the time and with Samantha's arms in casts, she can't take care of herself, let alone Billy. The doctor says she should be able to have the casts removed in six to eight weeks."

"Weeks? You mean… they will be there for two months?"

"I know this isn't what either of us wants, but I can't help it. I can't leave Billy to fend for himself and he's not capable of taking care of his mom."

"Well, if I didn't know better, I'd think she planned all this." Steam is rising under my collar.

"Darci! That's not like you," Brian says, gently.

"I can't help it. She has a way of sabotaging us every time we are loving life. And the other thing is, I don't know why you think it's best if we don't come to tend Mattie and Ethan's ponies while they're there. The kids will be heartbroken!"

"Just explain to them that I'll take care of them until—the house guests can leave. You know as well as I do, if we were all together, it wouldn't be good. Just having you here with her... you know how she is. She'd say or do things that will make you mad."

"I don't know how she could make me any more mad than I am, presently. Well, at least your parents are there. I hope Samantha doesn't upset them while they're visiting."

The phone goes quiet.

"Brian? They are there, aren't they?"

"They are leaving in about an hour. Rita is fixing everyone a late breakfast and then they'll be going."

"I thought you said they were staying at least a week for the holidays."

"They—changed their minds."

"I see. So, they aren't in favor with you tending to Billy and Samantha, am I right?"

His sigh says it all.

"They know it would be best if they left before I bring Samantha home. They doctor says she will be released in the morning."

It feels like someone just kicked me in my stomach. Bring. Samantha. Home. Those words echo in my mind.

"I need to go for a bit and spend a few minutes with Mom and Dad. I'll call you back later, okay?"

As much as I want to say *okay*, I don't. "No, Brian. That's not okay. You want me and the kids to stay away from the ranch while you have Samantha and Billy there for *two months*. The same woman who has tried everything in her power to tear us apart and *now* you are welcoming her into your home with open arms. No, Brian. It is far from okay. I don't know how I'm going to explain this to Mattie and Ethan about not going to take care of their ponies, let alone not getting to come see you at the cabin, but I'll find a way. Don't call me, Brian. There isn't a thing I want to hear from you."

If I could have slammed my mobile phone, I would have. I just hold the disconnected phone in my hand staring at it. Two months? It might as well be two years. I'm so mad at myself, I could spit nails. I *knew* better than getting my hopes up again. And now, I not only have to come up with a way to explain it to Mattie and Ethan, but I also have to tell mom and dad. Running a hand down my face, I slowly shake my head. Life just isn't fair!

CHAPTER 21

About four o'clock, mom calls. I hold my breath waiting for the next ax to fall.

"Hi, mom."

"Hi, honey. Listen, if you don't have other plans, I'm heating up leftovers and it's too much for your dad and myself. Would you and the kids like to come for dinner? Say, in an hour?"

"Mom, that would be wonderful. I really don't feel like cooking and I don't have any delicious Christmas goodies to prepare. The kids and I would love to share dinner with you. I'll get them out of their jammies and we'll head over."

"Nonsense. Let them stay in their jammies. I'm sure after a full belly they'll be ready to go to sleep all over again. At least we'll have no more snowstorms to worry about. Come whenever you're ready."

"Thanks, mom. We'll be there in just a bit."

I say goodbye and stare at my phone. A tear trinkles down my cheek. I swear a mother knows when her child needs her mom. That call feels like a hug I've been needing ever since I spoke to Brian. My chin trembles a bit. I know now that I want to fall into mom's arms and tell her all of my woes. I can forget about having to be strong for my children and forget about making sure everyone knows I have it all together. For just a while, I can be my mother's child and know, no matter what, she still loves me and will always be there for me. I'm not sure yet on how I'll tell her, especially with Mattie and Ethan with me, but I'll figure out a way. Grabbing a tissue, I dab my eyes and nose and put on a smile as I step into the living room over and through the toys strung all about.

"Guess what? Grandma and Grandpa want us to come over for dinner. They still have lots of our favorites. Doesn't that sound good?"

"Yes!" Mattie and Ethan say in unison.

"We don't even have to change, we'll go as we are. How about that? Now, run and grab your coats and we'll be on our way."

"Mommy, can I wear my warm new cape?"

"Of course, Mattie. That will be perfect. And before you ask Ethan, yes to the cowboy hat and new coat." I can't help but smile. Their cheers light up a light in my heart that I thought had gone out.

Donned in cape and jackets, we head for the door. I can't help but think I've been thrown a lifeline. Instead of being at home without a thing to do except think about Brian and the complications in life, we have something better to do. I open the door to a brisk wind and lift Ethan to my arms before we hurry to the car. Out of the corner of my eye, I notice Rita's front curtain move. I try not to think of the days ahead. The ones where Rita will inevitably ask me to reconsider waiting for Brian. No room for those thoughts today, or *ever*, if I have the strength to stand my ground.

We arrive at mom and dad's and darkness has already covered the lawn and their Christmas lights are glowing brightly. A nice reminder that life goes on. The front door swings open and my dad is standing there with a smile that won't end. I chuckle to myself, we were just there yesterday and he looks like we haven't been to see them in a month.

He scoops up Ethan and ushers Mattie inside with his other arm. Mom stands just inside the door ready to remove coats and hats. I remind myself how fortunate I am. Moving back close to mom and dad is the best thing in the world I could have done when Greg and I divorced. Greg—that's one person that will be happy as a lark when he finds out Brian and I fell apart. Just the mere thought of him is like biting into a lemon.

"I hope we didn't get here too early."

"Honey, you could stay here forever and we wouldn't mind, you know that. But—"

She sneaks a look at my dad, the children and then back to me. It's that look, you know the one where it looks like someone just swallowed a bird? Yes, *that* look.

"We do have an unexpected surprise for the children in the living room. Come on and see!"

The kids, of course, race into the living room with us following close behind. In front of the Christmas tree stands a box with bows all over the outside of its plain cardboard box.

Dad says, "Mattie, Ethan, come take a look."

They cluster around my dad and peer over the top of the box. I'm intrigued now and get there just as Mattie exclaims.

"Look, mommy! Kittens!"

Dad leans over and pulls out a white kitten with a black face and tail and hands it to Mattie. "I call this one Dancer, after Santa's reindeer. I'll tell you why in a minute."

"Oh, Grandpa, she's beautiful!" Mattie has that little thing right up in her face, rubbing her nose in its fur.

"And for you, Ethan, here is Prancer." He hands the little grey striped ball of fur to Ethan and he snuggles it close to his chest.

I'm surprised since mom and dad never really liked cats. They are more of dog lovers, if anything. I guess they felt the need to get the kids animals since they got ponies for Christmas…

"Now, let me tell you how we come to have these sweet little balls of fur. Your mother sent me up to the store to get us some more milk. Oh, it's a mess in that parking lot. All the snow has turned to a brownish mush from so many tires mashing it up.

Anyway, I hurried inside to grab the milk and a few extra things…"

"You know your father, he can't go to the store without coming home with a cart of goodies," mom says, laughing.

"Anyway, as I'm putting my groceries into the trunk, I hear crying. I look around and don't see anyone, but just as I was to get into the car, I hear it again. Well, by this time, I'm really concerned. I start looking into car windows and around the cars and truck thinking a child is out here without their parent. I get down on my knees at the truck in front of me and there I see them… two lone kittens huddled together in all that slushie snow, shivering up a storm! I reach out to get that little white one you're holding Mattie, and as scared as she was, she kept dancing away from my hand when I tried to reach her. Now Ethan, that kitty I call Prancer was completely different. When I reached as far as I could, that little grey ball of fur pranced himself right over to my hand, swishing his long wet tail every which way. Once I had him in my hands, I put him in the car so I could go back for the white kitten. When I bent over to try to get her, she was gone."

"Oh no, Grandpa. How did you find her?" Mattie asks.

"The funniest thing happened. I looked and looked under the truck and couldn't find her. I turned this way and that, and no little white kitten. I finally stood up and shrugged. There was nothing more I could do if she ran off, but as I turned to go to my car, I almost stepped on her. She was a shadow to my shoes. I reached down and snatched her up and brought her to be with her brother. Oh, they were a mess, indeed. Grandma fixed them right up with a warm bath and a thorough drying off. I think Dancer is at least two shades of white lighter than when I found her."

"Whatcha going to do with them, Grandpa?" Mattie asks, her face still buried deep into kitty fur.

He stands up, looking at my mother and then to me. "Well, these kittens are yours. If you want them to stay here, we will take care of them until you come over, or if your mother says it's okay…"

"Yes! They can have the kittens and bring them home!"

I'm practically in tears and I'm sure no one else knows why, but what dad did was give my children something to hold onto, something completely theirs without having to go somewhere else to enjoy them. I struggle to swallow tears wanting to come loose, tilting my head upward and whispering a thank you to the heavens. If this isn't a miracle, I wouldn't know one if it bit me. I hug the breath out of my dad and he's more than a bit surprised at my excitement. I look through watery eyes at my children, rolling around on the floor, playing with their new kittens. I can't help but feel someone up there is looking after us. How else could these two kittens show up right when we needed them most? All of a sudden a wave of chills, followed by a deep warmth, spreads over me. I look back at my dad. How in the world did he hear such small kittens in the first place? I have to speak louder than normal for him to even hear me. I feel down to my bones this is a special miracle created for Mattie and Ethan, as well as for me. For the first time in hours, I'm able to count my blessings and know I have more blessings than failures.

"Thank you, dad and mom. This means the world to us." I give them both a heartfelt hug. The look on their faces tells me they want to say something about the little furballs not being like getting ponies for Christmas, but for some reason they don't say such things. They just wrap their arms around me as we watch Mattie and Ethan enjoying the kittens.

Helping mom in the kitchen feels like the good old days. Everything feels nostalgic. Maybe it's the season of the year, or maybe it's me thankful to have the parents I do, who come wrapped up in foresight, ready to help their daughter again as in those times long ago with scraped knees, the first broken heart, and then the divorce. It makes me wonder how others get through such traumatic affairs without their parents to lean against. I think if I would have had to go through something like my divorce without them, I would have shattered into a million pieces. Sometimes we only look strong to those on the outside, but we really are fragile little teacups balanced precariously on the edge of the table.

Dinner is bites of warmth between even warmer laughter. I can't believe how wonderful the afternoon and night are. Being in my parents' home is giving me a new hope.

"Mom? Would it be okay for us to stay the night? It's been such a wearing day and a lovely evening."

"Oh, child, of course. Nothing would make us happier. You know your rooms are always ready. It's a delightful idea."

"Thanks, mom. The kids will tire out soon and I'm not prepared to take the kittens home and you know Mattie, she'll be crying up a storm in nothing flat."

"Come, we'll get the kids bedroom ready for them and the kittens. That will assure them a sweet night."

I wrap my arm through mom's and follow her to the bedrooms. Maybe after tucking Mattie and Ethan fall asleep, I'll have the nerve to tell her what's happened between Brian, myself, and the story behind the woman who had the accident last night.

After we get the children to bed, I stall between the hallway and my designated bedroom. Mom continues chatting to me and turns to discover I'm not with her. Tilting her head with the unspoken question, she comes back to where I am.

"Do you want to talk about it?"

I blink a few times in confusion and say, "Talk about what?"

"Oh, sweetie. There is something needling you, somewhere deep. I sensed it during our phone call."

"Mom, everything is going terrible!"

She doesn't say anything, she simply wraps me in her arms and pulls me close. All the bravery I thought I had clothed myself in vanishes. The tears flow and I'm sniffling against her shoulder. She does something she hasn't done in years and slowly runs her fingers through my hair. As a child this simple movement helped calm me and it's working now, too. I break apart from her and ask her to come into my room.

"I don't know where to begin, mom. I think I've fallen in love with Brian."

She gives me a loving, soft smile, but holds back her words sensing there is more I need to tell her. She's right.

"I know we all have a history, baggage that follows us around and Brian is no different. He had a relationship with a woman for several years. They actually lived with him."

"They?" Mom asks, confused.

"Her and her son. Anyway, the way Brian tells it is she was terrible for him and what made it worse is he fell in love with the boy as much as the woman. One day she decides the country life isn't for her, packs their bags and leaves Brian a note saying goodbye."

"Gracious! That's just terrible," mom says.

"It was really hard on him, but with enough time, he got over her. She tries to manipulate him at every chance. Mom, this woman is the one from the accident. Her name is Samantha."

"Oh, sweetie. I had no idea. I'm really sorry to have mentioned all of that to you." Mom's eyes are wide with surprise.

"It's okay, mom. You see, the kids and I had stayed over at Brian's house Christmas night. No need to raise your brows, mom, his parents and sister also were there. Anyway, I heard some shuffling around very early in the morning and got up. That's when I heard his sister and my neighbor, Rita, talking to Brian's mom, Connie. They had been called about Samantha's accident. She's broken both of her arms and needs help while she's in her cast. Brian—well, he's taking on the responsibility of caring for her and her son, Billy, at his house."

"She doesn't have family?"

"Well, her mother lives here, but from what I'm told, she works too much to be able to be there for her daughter all day and night. That is why Brian says he's taking them to his cabin."

Mom's face looks like a fish gulping for air. I can totally understand that look.

"What makes this even worse is Brian knows we don't get along. That's another long story having to do with the Christmas Extravaganza, but because of it, he doesn't think me and the children should visit the cabin while she and Billy are there. Mom, they'll be there like two whole months!"

Mom's hands land on each side of her face as her jaw drops.

"No wonder you were needing to come home, Darci. I don't know who I'd be more upset with, Brian or Samantha. How can he ask you not to go to the ranch? The children's ponies are there, for gracious sakes! Did he even think how hard this will hit them by not going to see their ponies?"

"I know. I haven't told them yet. I just don't know how to say it. That's why those kittens dad brought home for them… well, I think of it as a miracle. At least they will have Dancer and Prancer to pour their love into."

"It really is a miracle. You know your dad and I are more fond of dogs than cats, but for some reason, they showed up for your dad and he felt compelled to help them out. Now, I know why they chose your dad to find them. They needed someone just as the children will need them. I'm so sorry, Darci. It really is a mess, isn't it?"

I nod. My fingers go to the soft throw on the bed and start picking at the tassels. It goes quiet before the storm.

"Well, I daresay you aren't going to let either of them tell you that you can't bring Mattie and Ethan to tend to their ponies, are you? Brian is the one that arranged things to be this way by giving them the ponies in the first place, knowing they had no place to keep them except at his place. Now, he has the audacity to expect you and the children to stay away while he plays nursemaid to his ex? Hogwash, I say!"

I'm astounded. I would never have believe my mom would take this stance, nor be so upset with what I am telling her. I scratch the side of my face, thinking.

"I'll tell you what we're going to do. Tomorrow morning, we're going to have our breakfast, then we're going to do what we had planned to do, by having the children show us their Christmas ponies as they feed them!"

"Mother, we can't do that. Not when Brian has already asked us not to come to his place."

"Of course you can and you will. He will not crush my grandchildren's heart, not without me being there to tell him what a jerk he is being. He decided to bring her and her son into his home after he already made promises to you and my grandchildren, promises where he declared they could come to the ranch at any time to see and care for their ponies… not just at his convenience." She huffs what should be smoke fuming from her mouth.

"Well, we probably could get there before he gets back from the hospital with Samantha and Billy. I'm sure they will have to stop at her mother's for clothes and whatever."

"Perhaps, but I'm sure they will return while we are still enjoying the ponies. Of that, I have no doubt."

"Mother!"

"What? No one is going to set up rules for my daughter and grandchildren after going out of their way to keep them close to his ranch. No, he should have thought this out better if he had thoughts of playing nursemaid to another woman and her child. So what if this Samantha doesn't like it. Why should he even consider what she would like or not? He already knows how she treated him like an afterthought. I'm surprised that you haven't already straightened him out on this. I'm not saying that we are going there to start a disagreement, but we are going there by means of his promise to you and your children. Make no mistake about that. He isn't going to be pulling the strings on my grandchildren's happiness."

Well, this isn't what I expected by telling mom my heartache, but… she's right in everything she said. Brian did make promises to both myself and my children. I'm not going to crush their hearts just to make life easier around Samantha. And really, when you think about it, she doesn't have to even see us while we are there. She can stay in the cabin while we go out to the stables to take care of the ponies. If she wants to get out and butt into our lives, that will be her problem. I feel like I finally have unwound. I give mom the biggest hug I can and say my goodnight. I think I'll actually be able to sleep tonight.

CHAPTER 22

Butterflies flutter in my stomach as I crawl out of bed. Last night everything felt right, to go to Brian's ranch and give the children their right to tend to their own ponies, but today—today it makes me anxious. I dislike confrontation and would prefer not seeing Brian at all, now that he feels the need to allow Samantha and Billy not only back in his house, but back into his life. I know enough about Samantha in this short time to recognize what she will be working on and it will be to make her stay permanent. If it wasn't for my children, I'd just as soon let Brian go his own way and the sooner the better. I want a drama free life and it won't ever happen with Samantha around.

Opening my door, the aroma of fresh coffee and bacon tickles my nose. I peek into the room where Mattie and Ethan slept, and the beds are empty. A smile crosses my lips. Their kittens are missing, too. Those little puffs of fur and love must be playing with the children downstairs.

The sound of their laughter reaches me before I hit the bottom step, giving me the resolve to go through with taking the children to feed and love on their ponies and show them off to their Grandparents. Stepping into the living room, my eardrums are assaulted with both Mattie and Ethan telling me every little thing Dancer and Prancer have done and are currently doing. I tousle their hair and give them smooches before heading to the kitchen to infuse myself with coffee.

Mom grins, pours me a cup of that wonderful elixir, and passes it to me over the bar before going back to remove the bacon from the skillet. I sneak a piece from the platter, earning me a swift hand slap and a chuckle. The game never grows old. I have done the same thing since childhood. I look at the assortment of platters, softly shaking my head. Biscuits, hash browns, bacon, and now the eggs are being scrambled. My ready stomach growls.

"I thought I might as well make the whole nine-yards since we don't know how long we'll be tending to our grandchildren's ponies." The gleam in her eye isn't missed. "Of course, we want to see them ride their ponies." And there it is, the smile of a Cheshire cat. I almost spew my mouthful of coffee.

"Well, we'll see, mom. I haven't saddled the ponies before and I'm not sure I want to do that by myself."

"Oh, posh. Your dad can do that. He's saddled many a horse in his day, the ponies won't be a problem for him." She scoops the scrambled eggs onto the remaining platter, handing it to me to set on the table.

I know I'm wearing a smirk. I remember clearly in my growing-up days that when mom made up her mind about something, there was no changing it. This definitely feels like one of those lines in the sand. The children *will* be riding their ponies, come what may. Good thing we'll have our stomachs full… I'm sure we won't be in any hurry to leave the ranch. I'm just as sure mom will make sure we are there when Brian brings Samantha to the ranch. I'm thankful they will be with me, I can't imagine going to Brian's ranch by myself with the children. At least, not the first time after he has asked us to stay away.

The breakfast table is full of excitement and chatter, not to mention all the great food. Isn't it funny how I can make the same food, but it always tastes better when mom makes it? Leaning back into my chair, I drain the last dregs of coffee from my cup and let the food settle. Motion catches my attention out the window. Mom's breakfast table windows face the side of their yard. You would think the squirrels are nestled deep into their little homes, but not around mom and dad's place. They keep a bowl full of nuts and berries to make sure the little critters don't wither away over winter. It's quite comical watching them scampering through the snow and loading their cheeks with as much as they can carry back to their den in the tree.

It just occurs to me, I've let Mattie and Ethan stay in their jammies. I need to take them home to change before heading to Brian's ranch because they won't be warm enough with all the snow outside. After clearing the table, I let mom know.

"I'll tell you what. Get a head start to your house and get the children wrapped up in warmth. We'll head to your place in a bit. We'll take the SUV today so we can all fit. I'll just do a quick-change and rustle the dishes into the dishwasher and then we'll be right behind you, okay?"

"That will be great, mom. We'll see you in a bit. Oh, can we leave the kittens here until we get back? I have to set up a place for them yet at the house."

"Of course! We'll keep them in the children's *stay-over* room since all their necessities are already in there. When we're all done at the ranch, we'll drop you off first so you can get ready for your new family additions, and then we'll bring them over. How's that sound?"

"Perfect, as always, mom. I really appreciate it."

"Anything for you and our grandchildren," she answers, smiling.

I rustle up the kids, now filled to the brim with breakfast, and tell them we'll have the kitties home after we get done with their ponies today. That helps quell their protests of having to leave without them clutched to their chests. Now I can slip them into their jacket, cape and hats, and usher them out to the car. The short drive is filled with excitement. Theirs. Mine, not so much. I still have butterflies trying to escape my stomach. I want so much for the trip to be enjoyable and the thought of Brian, Samantha, and Billy makes it hard to keep happy thoughts.

After I park the car, I get Mattie out first, then Ethan. I lift Ethan into my arm and latch hold of Mattie's hand as we crunch through the snow to get to our door. I waste no time unlocking the door and hurrying them inside. For one thing, I don't want to meet Rita outside and spill the beans about what we are doing. I have no doubt she will find out in short order.

I lay out the clothes for Mattie and Ethan and rush to my bedroom to switch out of my cozy sweats and into my thermals, jeans, and a bright blue sweater with my jacket and neck scarf. It almost matches the one I made Brian… oh well. I finish getting Ethan ready when I hear a knock on the door. I bite my lip. I wonder, is it mom or Rita? I tiptoe into the living room and look through the peephole. Thank goodness, it's mom.

"Come inside, mom. We're almost ready." Bending over, I grab the discarded cape and leather jacket and have them ready for them as they rush to their grandmother. She is ready with the hats. "Oh, my hat. I'll be right back." I dodge back to my room, glancing around to see where I laid it. There it is, on the vanity. I grab it up and knock something onto the floor. Bending down, I pick it up. A deep sigh gushes out. It's the necklace Brian gave me, the one with the tiny reindeer. I stare at it for a long minute and set it back in its place. I can't believe how much has changed in a day or two. I frown. If it hadn't been for those stinking reindeer, I would never have gotten all wrapped into Brian's world. I touch the necklace one last time.

"Darci, are you ready?"

"Coming, mom."

We stomp through the compacted snow and climb into the back seat of the SUV. Dad is grinning up a storm. If I could see mom's face from my seat, I'm sure it matches his.

"Are we all buckled up and ready to go?" He looks into his rearview mirror, watching our heads bob as we answer, "Yes!"

"Then, here we go! Darci, feed me the directions as we go, dear."

"No problem. It's an easy find, once you know how to get there."

Looking at me in the rearview mirror, his brow arches. "That's good to know. I never have a problem finding a place, once I've been there." There's a lot said in his look. No added words are necessary.

"That road right there, Grandpa. That leads up to the cabin," Mattie says, enthusiastically.

Dad steers the SUV onto the road. We only go a short distance until the gate starts to come into view. I forgot about the gate. What if the code to open it has changed? No need to wonder any longer, the gate is wide open. I wonder if that means they have returned to the ranch? Mercy, the butterflies have flown and left my stomach to pitch and turn. What have we gotten ourselves into?

I hear mom gasp when she sees Brian's cabin. I want to snicker because it's the same reaction I had, besides thinking I was completely lost. Dad clears his throat.

"So, this is the cabin, is it?"

"Yes, dad. That's what Brian calls it. The cabin. It's really not an overkill when you see inside, mainly everything is just stretched out a bit more."

"You don't say." Dad's bushy brow is raised as he stares at me in the rearview mirror.

I don't know why my palms are sweating so. It makes me feel like I have a guy coming over to meet my parents. Well, I guess if Brian comes home while we are still here, that's exactly what it will be like. I didn't really think this part out.

"Where should I park?"

I lean forward and point. "Over there by the barns. Brian won't recognize your car, of course, but I want it in plain sight so he won't think there is something shifty going on."

This elicits a genuine giggle from mom. A giggle.

"Hurry up, Grandpa. I can't wait to show you my pony," says Mattie, bouncing on the seat.

"Me too," Ethan joins in.

Dad finally parks the car. I get out and unbuckle both Mattie and Ethan from their car seats and help them out of the car. Mattie dodges over to Grandma's car door and flings it wide open, grabbing at her hand.

"Come on, Grandma. I bet you've never seen ponies as pretty as the ones we have," Mattie says confidently as she tugs at my mom's hand.

"Isn't this exciting? I can't wait to see them—and everything else." Mom smiles at Mattie, but I see a shark swimming in the shallows. All I can say is Samantha better not get smart with mom, she won't know what bit her until it's too late. I chuckle under my breath. That's a rather good image I have in my mind.

Grandpa has Ethan by his hand and Mattie has Grandma. I walk slowly behind them, allowing the kids to do all the show and tell. The excitement on everyone's faces makes me smile, too. It's been a long time since the kids had anything this exciting to show their grandparents and I can't tell who is enjoying it the most. We stop at the pen that has several of the ponies milling around. They are still eating an assortment of carrots and apples Brian must have left for them before going to the hospital. We don't stay there long, the kids are too electrified to remain with the other ponies.

We first stop at Bella's stall. I get a lump in my throat. Brian also has Bella a bucket of food topped off with sliced apples. On the side of the stall next to Bella's name is a sign. Mattie's pony. It is a wooden sign that has been chiseled out just to leave the words. Running over the top of the stall is a thick garland of evergreens tied in places with red bows. Tears threaten to fall. I'm suddenly thrust back into hearing what's going on around me. Mom and dad are tickled pink to be sharing this time with the kids. I am too, I only wish it would be under better circumstances.

Ethan won't hold still. He begs my mom and dad to hurry and come see his pony, because as pretty as Bella is, Dark Knight is even prettier, he assures them. I'm glad I never had to choose between the two ponies because they certainly are the pick of the litter, as they say.

Dark Knight knickers when he sees Ethan. Grandpa lifts Ethan up so he can pet him over the stall door. Dark Knight's stall is set up the very same way as Bella's is, complete with the engraved sign stating that Dark Knight is Ethan's pony. I'm trying so hard not to think of the extra touches Brian has done to make their ponies' stalls special and different. I bite on the inside of my lip to keep me from tearing up.

"I don't think I've ever seen as nice ponies anywhere. You both are very lucky to have been given such a gift," dad says, smiling at the two of them.

"Hey! Who's back here?" a deep and startled voice calls out.

I whirl my head, knowing full well who the voice belongs to.

"Brian, It's us. Darci, Mattie, and Ethan. They wanted to show their grandparents their ponies."

He rounds the corner with a shovel clutched in his hand.

"Darci?" He stops and stares. His words are slow to come to the realization of who all is in the barn. "Uh, hi. I didn't expect to see you today."

"I know. But the kids wanted to see their ponies and show them off to their grandparents. "Brian, this is my dad, Walter Grisbane and my mother, Jillian Grisbane."

Brian leans the shovel against the wall and walks forward, confusion still playing across his face. "Hello, Mr. and Mrs. Grisbane. What an unexpected surprise. I'm Brian Walters." He extends his hand to my dad, who takes a hair longer before extending his hand.

"Brian, nice to meet you. We're sorry to just drop by like this, but it was upon our grandchildren's insistence. They are so proud of those ponies you so generously gifted them."

"Thank you, sir. I was glad to do it. They actually did me a favor. I love these ponies and although there are plenty here, there are none as sweet as these two. Now they'll remain here and Mattie and Ethan will treat them the way they should be treated, with lots of petting, hugs, and love."

"We sure will, Brian!" Mattie answers.

"It's a shame. You just missed my parents. They would have enjoyed meeting you," Brian says with a soft smile.

I'm beginning to think I have all of this pent-up worry for nothing. I begin to relax and enjoy Brian talking to my dad. I can see he's being sincere and it makes my heart race a bit. He moves over to my mom and shakes her hand also.

"Brian! Brian! Where are you?"

And now, my stomach drops to the floor.

"Back here, Billy. We have… guests."

Billy rushes around the corner and comes to a screeching halt. "Hey, I know you! You were at the hayride."

Mattie and Ethan go over to Billy and start chatting.

"What are you guys doing out here?" Billy asks.

"We are here to see our ponies and show them to Grandpa and Grandma. Have you seen them, Billy? Brian is just the best! He gave us Bella and Dark Knight!"

His jaw drops as he turns to look at Brian.

"That's right, Billy. They are a perfect fit for Mattie and Ethan."

"Uh, mom is wondering where you went. She needs your help settling in. She doesn't know where I'm supposed to put her luggage and all."

"I'll be there in a moment, Billy. Go on, you can help her settle on the couch for now. I planned on bringing one of the beds down and set it up in my study, but since she was released earlier than expected. I haven't gotten that far yet."

"Oh, okay. Do you want me to put my stuff in my old room?"

"We'll figure it out when I get to the cabin. Let me get them situated out here and I'll be inside soon."

"Okay, but you know how mom gets when she has to wait."

"I'll be there… soon," Brian says as a flush rises to his face.

"See you guys later," Billy says, waving at Mattie and Ethan before taking off in a trot.

Brian turns and looks at me and then to my parents. "I'm sorry about that. His mother had an accident the other evening and they have nowhere else to go to be taken care of, you see. So, they'll be staying here for a bit."

"We're sorry to intrude. It looks like you have your hands full, Brian. Say, why don't I come up to the house with you and help you relocate that bed?"

"Oh, no, sir. I couldn't ask you to do that."

My dad claps Brian solidly on his shoulder. "You didn't ask, Brian. I offered. I'll tell you what—you pitch in and help me saddle up these ponies for Mattie and Ethan, and I'll go back with you to lend you a hand."

The look on Brian's face is priceless. He knows he's cornered, and to remain in good graces he'll have to accept or lose face with my father, in front of me and the kids. "I'll be glad to help saddle the ponies up. Come on, I'll show you where I keep the saddles for them." As they saunter off, mom comes to my side.

"I think that went very well, don't you?" I swear she's purring like a kitten. She leans in and whispers to me, "And, your Brian is a handsome man. Full of manners, too. Hard to find someone like him in this day and age."

I know I must be all shades of crimson. I hear dad and Brian rounding the corner and I walk Mattie back to Bella's stall. It gives me just enough time to push my blush back down before Brian or my dad can see it. It doesn't take but a few minutes to get Bella ready for a ride. Brian escorts Bella to Dark Knight's stall and ties her to the next gate as they prepare Ethan's pony.

"Darci, did you want them to ride around in the round pen?" Brian asks.

"Yes, that will be perfect. I can open the gate. Why don't you and dad go take care of what you need to. Mom and I can take care of Mattie and Ethan as they ride. Thank you again for the wonderful gifts," I say, trying to sound cordial. It takes him by surprise and he shuffles from foot to foot. Dad has to break the silence.

"Well, they're good to go. Let's go get that bed." Dad spins and takes a step before Brian can catch up.

After they've walked off a few paces, we return our attention to Mattie and Ethan, who are anxious to get on their ponies. We get them situated and I tell them to hold the reins as mom and I guide them to the round pen. Mom guides Mattie and I guide Ethan. The ponies are excited to be with us and knicker up a storm. We're laughing in no time at all, simply enjoying the fun we're having with them. But, my oh my, how I wish I could be a mouse in dad's pocket as he walks inside the cabin with Brian. I bet Samantha is fit to be tied after I'm sure Billy filled her in on who's out in the barn and that Brian didn't drop everything and race back to meet her immediate "needs."

CHAPTER 23

I glance at my wristwatch and realize we've been here for over two hours. You can't tell it by Mattie and Ethan, they are having the time of their lives and, I daresay, so is Grandma. She's taken so many pictures on her phone, she's probably completely out of space. I look back to the barn and don't see dad yet. That sends another wave of butterflies swarming my stomach.

"Okay, you two. Time to get Bella and Dark Knight back to their stalls. I'm sure they need a nice long rest after all of that walking they did." I expected moans and groans and am pleasantly surprised when all they can do is ask their Grandma if she had fun watching them ride. She'll probably regret all the walking tomorrow, but for today she's in paradise. After we get the ponies near their stalls, I manage to get Mattie down and remove the saddle from Bella. I slip her into her stall and then work on getting Ethan down and the saddle removed from Dark Knight. Once he's back in his stall, I feel better.

"Aw, poor Grandpa. He missed watching us ride our ponies. I hope he won't feel too bad when he sees we've put them away." Mattie frowns.

"Don't you worry none for your Grandpa," mom says. "I bet there will be plenty of more chances for him to watch you ride."

Mattie nods and grins. "You're right, Grandma. We can do this whenever we want to."

I hope those words don't come back to haunt me. I'm a bit worried dad hasn't returned yet. I can't help but chew on the inside of my cheek, wondering. When he still doesn't make it back to the barn by the time we've watered the ponies, my stomach starts twisting in knots.

"What should we do, mom?"

"There's only one thing *to* do. We drive up to the cabin and see if he's ready to leave." She says it so pragmatically, I'm left without words to say.

"Come on, dear. Let's go get your father."

After buckling the children in their car seats, I climb in front and mom drives up to the cabin. I'm hoping that dad or even Brian will see we've pulled up and come outside. We sit for what seems to be hours, waiting. Okay, so a few minutes pass, but where is my dad?

"Darci, be a dear and see if your father is ready to leave." She looks at me smiling, this time not like a Cheshire cat but as a mom giving clear directions to her daughter. I sigh and open the car door. I slowly climb the steps to the porch still hoping they will come outside. No such luck.

Knocking on the door, I wait. I hear Samantha.

"Billy, go see who's at the door. I guess today it's going to be like Grand Central Station."

He opens the door and just stands there.

"Hi, Billy. Can you tell me where my dad went?"

"Oh, sure. He's in the study with Brian. Come on in."

I cross the threshold and see Samantha narrow her eyes.

"I heard about your accident, Samantha. I'm so sorry your Christmas evening was spent in the hospital." Although the sentiment is true, it still leaves a nasty taste in my mouth.

"Hello again, Darla," she says, dripping poisonous honey on each word. I don't even correct her on the name. We both know she knows what my name is. "I hear Brian gave your kids horses. That man, I'll tell you, always giving to the less fortunate ones."

"He is, at that. I remember Billy telling us all about the animals Brian gave him." I smile cordially to her, even though her cheeks have puffed up like one of those puffer fish. I like the mental image that gives me so I smile an even bigger smile as I walk to the study.

"Dad, we were getting worried. We've already put the ponies in their stalls and we're just waiting for you."

"I'm so sorry. I got caught up with talking to Brian as we carried the bed and frame down to his study. I must apologize, Brian, for taking up so much of your time today."

"No, I really appreciate the help, Walt. It's been nice talking with you."

"Darci, I'm sorry I kept him away from watching Mattie and Ethan ride today. He's really been a big help. I don't know how I would have gotten everything down here by myself. Maybe you could bring the kids back out tomorrow afternoon for a ride?"

"I don't know, Brian. We'll see. We really don't want to be intruding while you have… guests."

He looks down at his boots for a moment then straight into my eyes. "I was wrong, Darci. I shouldn't have suggested you wait to bring the kids over until Samantha gets better. I see that now. It really is no bother to have you here."

I can't help it, a smile betrays me. Enough so that Brian smiles right back at me, causing a whole other set of butterflies to stir. This is the kind I like. A lot. "Let me see how they're feeling tomorrow. They've been in the saddle a long time today," I say, chuckling. "They may not be up to it."

"I'll understand if that's why. You'll call, won't you? To let me know? I don't imagine we'll be going anywhere."

"Uh, yeah. I'll let you know one way or the other. Are you ready, dad?" I suddenly feel claustrophobic. Everything is getting mixed up. I thought I knew what to do, but now, I'm not certain. He calls my dad Walt…

I hook my arm through dad's to pry him away from chitchatting with Brian. I don't give Samantha a second look. I know she must be seething after hearing Brian ask us over tomorrow. I think it's a perfect time to leave.

As we get into the car, I catch dad glancing at mom. He raises and wiggles his eyebrows. I wonder what that's all about but I'm afraid to ask with the kids in the car. Sometimes they may act like they aren't listening, but I'll tell you what, those little sponges hear and repeat everything—usually at the most inappropriate times.

"Were you able to help Brian bring the bed down?" Mom asks.

"Yes, indeed. Between the two of us, it wasn't much trouble. For a single man, there sure are a bunch of bedrooms in that house."

"How many?"

"I'm sure I must have seen five or six of them. All upstairs, too. We only brought down the mattresses and bed frame, leaving the bulky stuff behind. After our third load coming down the stairs, I told Brian I probably would have opted to go buy one of those blow-up beds. You should have heard him laugh, as if it was the funniest thing ever said."

"Hmm, I bet to him, it probably was," Mom says, chuckling under the palm of her hand.

"What did the two of you find to talk about all that time?" I ask.

His large brown eyes meet mine in the rearview mirror. "Oh, this and that. You know how it goes, one topic leads to another. Say, do you recall the *Therapy House*? It's the quaint Victorian looking affair not far from the main part of town. Mother and I went to their ribbon cutting several years back, you know, to keep in mind services we may yet need one day. Anyway, it just occurred to me while I was talking to Brian that we have such wonderful amenities in our small town of Hope Falls. I'm not sure how long he has lived here, but he seemed truly surprised to hear of it, especially the fact that it is family orientated. I told him that was the part that impressed me the most, knowing if I or your mother, ever had a serious injury that we needed help, neither of us would be separated from the other." He reaches over and pats mom's hand, giving her a loving smile.

When his eyes return to the rearview mirror, he catches my jaw dropping and shares a fatherly wink with me. Whether Brian pursues this avenue, I'll have to wait and see, but at least he knows that there are options. Great options. And, he will know that since dad spoke of it to him, I will be aware of the option, too. Of course, I have no idea what something like that would cost, especially considering the length of time Samantha will need around the clock care. Just hearing this part of their shared conversation has let hope flutter its tiny wings in my heart.

CHAPTER 24

By the time we reach our apartment, the kids are yawning up a storm. Knowing mom and dad will be back soon with the kittens, I remove our outer wear and perch Mattie and Ethan on the couch. I slip on a Christmas movie while they get comfortable. Looking over our small apartment, I decide the kitty litter box will be best in the children's bathroom since there is an open vanity space where it can sit inconspicuously. I have canned tuna to give them until I make a trip to the store. I sit at the table to make out a list of things we'll be needing for the next few days.

The phone rings and I snatch it up on the first ring expecting it to be mom. It's not. It's Samantha.

"Hello, Darla, this is Samantha. I hope you don't mind me calling. I really hate to be a bother, dear, but as you could see while you were here, I've had a great deal of damage from the accident. With both arms broken, well, I just can't do a thing for myself and Billy, poor soul, he is no help at all. Brian and I discussed this, bless his heart, he just couldn't find it in his heart to make the call. Anyway, it's best if you and your children don't return to the ranch. No worries, hon. Brian can feed those ponies. He just won't have the time to be pulled away doing frivolous things while I'm in this predicament. You understand, don't you, hon?"

I want to pull her through the phone. That's what I understand. "May I speak to Brian, please?"

"There is no need and besides, he and Billy are outside, you know, sugar, doing those boy things. Billy sure has missed his Brian, but he's happy as can be to be back home."

"Samantha, I don't believe a word of what you say, and won't unless Brian calls me himself and tells me the same thing. You're not near as sneaky as you think you are, Samantha, and I wouldn't put it past you that you had the 'accident' on purpose to weasel a place back with Brian. I can see what you are doing and using Billy is downright despicable! So, no, *hon*, I won't be listening to any more of your garbage. Have a great day!" I end the call.

My chest is hammering like I've been running. The nerve of her! I look at my phone again and block her number. I shake my head. This is only Day 1. And this could take six to eight weeks? There is no way I can be around that woman for that length of time.

Glancing over to the sofa, I note that the kids have fallen asleep. Thank goodness. I sure don't want to explain to them my phone call. I take a deep breath and hold it for a five count before letting it out. Little by little my heart slows its hammering and finds a slower rhythm. Rubbing my face with both hands, I try to wipe away the phone call, but it clings to me like the odor of a skunk. Now that's a fit description of her. She goes through life stinking up everything she passes. I look at my phone trying to decide if I should call Brian when there's a knock at the door.

I open it so see mom with her hands full of kittens and dad bringing up the rear with all the accessories they already have to Dancer and Prancer.

"Come in! The kids are asleep on the sofa, but you can sit here at the table," I say as I let them through the door.

"Where do you want the litter box and food bowls?" Dad is doing an amazing job of holding everything without dropping things.

"In the kids' bathroom, under the vanity," I say as he heads down the hallway. Mom sits down and lets the kittens go. They explore around our shoes and under the table. It gives me a smile to watch their furry cuteness as they scramble about. I sigh and mom's brows furrow in question.

"Oh, it's nothing, mom. Just, well, Samantha had the nerve to call me to tell me not to return to the ranch." I frown and roll my eyes.

"The devil you say!" she says, shocked.

"Right? She told me her and Brian discussed this issue and he was too tender-hearted to call me himself. When I asked to speak to him she gave some story of him and Billy being outside doing guy stuff together. Mom, I really don't want to create drama. But when we left everything seemed fine for us to come and go as we please. I certainly don't want Samantha dictating orders to me and my children."

"Have you called Brian, yet?"

"No, I barely hung up from her when you arrived."

"Say, what's going on in here? What's this about calling Brian?"

"Oh, dad. It's that Samantha. Evidently, she's unhappy that we were at the ranch and now says Brian and her had a discussion and it would be best if we stayed away while she is recovering. I'm almost sure he knows nothing of this phone call nor did they even have this so called discussion—but, I don't have the time or energy to be involved with all this drama. I mean, it's Winter break from school and soon Mattie will go back and Ethan will be at daycare, so they wouldn't be going out there except on weekends anyway…"

"I may not know everything that is going on, but I do know this. Brian feels like he's between a rock and a hard place and doesn't even know how he got there. He's doing what he thinks is right. He spoke about Samantha showing up before the accident. He feels guilty for arguing with her and thinks that is why she got into a wreck. I tried to tell him it wasn't, that she came looking for a fight and she knew she was uninvited, but he can only see the part where she left mad then wrecked. Darci, I can tell he has feelings for you and that is what is making this thing with Samantha so difficult."

"You know me, dad. I've never been one of those "it's either me or them" type of people, but I don't want to have to second guess everything. Even as sure as I am that Brian didn't say the things Samantha says he did, if I call and ask Brian, what does that do? Sure, it would open the door for us to continue going over, but at what cost? He'd go to Samantha and confront her with the call and she'd just find another way to make our visit to the ranch miserable. I don't want any of what Samantha is dishing out to touch Mattie and Ethan. It will happen before you know it."

"Honey, it's completely up to you whether you call Brian or not. I'm glad, however, that you realize he isn't the sort of man that would say or do the things Samantha indicated during her phone call to you. Just know your mother and I are on your side, whatever you decide. If you want to take a few days and see how things go, do so. Those ponies belong to Mattie and Ethan and before they get upset at not seeing them, I'll be the first to let you know, mother and I will take them there ourselves."

I hug my dad. He gives me strength to stand on my own two feet but always is there, right behind me, to catch me should I fall. "Thanks, dad. The kids had such a wonderful day out there today, I'm sure waiting at least a few days won't bother them too much. That will give me time to consider what would be best for our family."

He looks at the kittens snooping into every cubbyhole and smiles. "Dancer and Prancer should help them during this transition. I'm so glad they took to the kittens right away."

I laugh. "Well, you know your grandkids. They'd take to a spider on a leash if they saw one."

He chuckles. "That's probably the truth. Anyway, daughter, we had the most wonderful time with you today. I'm happy to have met Brian and have no doubt we'll see him sometime in the future. You call me if you need anything." He bends his head to look me straight in the eyes before continuing. "And I mean anything, you hear?"

"Yes, dad. You know I will. Thanks for everything. We're going to enjoy these puffs of fur so much. The kids are going to be beside themselves when they wake up and see the kittens running around."

"Okay, then. Come on, mother. Let's get back to the house and rest up. We both had more of a workout than we usually get."

"Bye, Darci, dear. Call if you need anything."

"I will, mom. Love you both."

After closing the door behind them, I slump down into the recliner. I'm very fortunate to have both of my parents so close to me and even more lucky that we have a great relationship. So many people miss out on that. I pull the blanket off the back of the recliner and cover up. A bit of rest can't hurt me any

CHAPTER 25

I'm awakened to the sound of giggles and kitty meows. As soon as I know the cats are not wiggling under the recliner, I sit up and watch the children play. After a few minutes, I try to decide what to tackle first, food or our small Christmas tree. Noticing the ornaments at the bottom have already been swatted off, it's the Christmas tree that gets my attention. Sending the children off to their bedroom, I'm free to set the boxes out on the couch to start bundling the ornaments away. Some of them are from when I was a little girl, so I'd like to keep them intact so I can pass them on to Mattie and Ethan.

I fill the boxes and replace them on the upper shelves in my closet, to wait until next year. I pause and stand there wondering, what next year will be like at Christmastime? I can't help it, I sigh deeply. There for a while, I thought it might still include Brian. I'm practically ashamed of myself, for building such hope up in such a short time. It isn't as if we have years invested in a relationship. It was just the beginning of something… cliché as it sounds, of something beautiful. I meander over to my vanity and pick up my Christmas necklace of the tiny silver reindeer with its red bow. I clutch it tightly in my palm remembering when Brian slipped it around my neck, remembering the kisses we shared. I shake myself out of it and put the necklace away in the drawer. At least I can say the children and I had a wonderful

Christmas and even enjoyed hayrides this year. No matter what, we have golden memories.

I decide there and then, I'm stepping away from Brian and the ranch. I'm going to take my dad up on him and mom taking the kids out on weekends to tend to their ponies. If Brian can't figure out why Samantha always gets the upper hand with him, then he's not the man I thought he was. The last thing I want in my life right now is another wishy-washy man. It feels good making up my mind. I feel a little ball of courage rise and lodge in my chest. The good thing is Mattie and Ethan, as much as they like Brian, never got to the point where they thought of him as someone in their future. He was just a good and kind man. Yes, and that's the way it's going to remain.

The morning comes with freezing rain. I'm glad we have no need to get out in this mess. At least, looking from the window, the Christmas lights still make a marvelous glow across the bushes and lawn. I finally have the house back into 'pre-Christmas' order and the kittens have explored and know the boundaries of their new home. They are like a ray of sunshine in our little place. I never would have thought bringing cats into our apartment would bring in so much love and delight.

At least I don't have to have the discussion about going out to feed the ponies. Mattie and Ethan were as pleased as could be to stay home in the warmth and play non-stop with Dancer and Prancer. It makes it easier for me, too. I still have a few last-minute calls to make for the New Year's Masquerade Ball being hosted by the city. It will be in the old hotel, *The Crimson Leaf.* It's the perfect venue for the party in which all the who's-who of town will come out. Tickets can either be purchased in advance or at the door with all of the proceeds going to a charity. This year's recipient for the charity will be *Just Beyond*. I personally love their work. It helps anyone that needs a bit of help beyond what their normal circumstances can provide. This includes graduating students wanting class pictures and rings, prom dresses and hairdos, single-income parents who need help with interview clothes, really, the list is endless and the charity is open to all that need help. I'm pleased part of my ticket purchase will go directly to this charity.

I have even thought of asking Brian if he would want to attend with me, but of course, not now. At any rate I'll be kept busy making sure everything goes off without a hitch. I'll be playing banker and will be close to the ticket tables in the beginning, helping to make change if necessary. The downstairs of the hotel is a gorgeous affair with all the old woodworking in turned banisters and a bar running down the full wall after the staircase. Above, on the first floor, is a veranda sweeping over the top of the bar where the band will set up to play music. Although the city of Hope Falls has rented the hotel as the venue for our Masquerade Ball, rooms can still be rented and drinks bought at the bar. The city provides the tables, the buffet meal, the noise makers, and remembrances to take home. Once this event is over, I can rest a bit before going in full-throttle for Valentine's Day.

Tomorrow I can run out there to make sure all the tables were delivered and the tablecloths ready to go. The florist has already called about the table arrangements. It will be such a delightful night to be a part of, even with no date. I'm glad I can leave Mattie and Ethan at mom and dad's overnight. They always try to make it awake to New Years, but rarely have made it. I'll miss not being with them, but it will be so fun trying to guess who is who with all the masks. I even splurged and bought myself a mask. Oh, not one of the dime store kind, a real masquerade type mask. It makes me giddy just looking at it. It goes perfect with my black and gold gown, The mask covering my entire face, and on one half of the mask is a black and gold butterfly wing, bedazzled with pearls. On the other half is white lace appliques with the pearl garnishments. The lips are outlined in gold, with silver being the color of the lips themselves. They have a small slit in them so I can be heard when speaking. I think after the party I will display it either on my wall or buy one of those heads for wigs and place it on there. It really is too beautiful to keep in a box in the gloominess of a closet. Just thinking of the party makes me feel like a kid again, wanting to play dress up. All of that can wait. I have things that must be done first.

Thank goodness, when I wake up I hear the trucks running to sand and salt the thoroughfares. It's a crisp and bright day and I can't wait to get started. Today, I'm taking Mattie and Ethan to mom's. I really shouldn't be in town too long, just long enough to see that deliveries are being made to *The Crimson Leaf.* I'll have to come back out Friday, in order to have the florist put the table arrangements where they go. Sometimes I think there should be at least two weeks between Christmas and New Years as far as an event planner goes! Friday will also be the day the balloons and confetti will be suspended over the tables and by the bar. They haven't had this event in the last four or five years because of all the coordination it requires with so many venders. It's a dream the way things are coming together, it even leaves me time to enjoy the romance of the whole thing… dreaming of my prince charming coming in to save the day… yeah, right! I shake my head at my own silliness, but it's not enough to dampen my mood. New Year's celebration is always fabulous. I love the idea of a clean slate, of making new goals and of looking at the world with a bit more magic than I do on every other day.

When I arrive at the hotel, the parking lot is filled with vans and trucks unloading what will go inside. The vendors get directions from the hotel manager as to where to put things. I admire the owners, the Wilhelms, for making the hotel available for this event. I can't think of another place that holds so much charm, elegance, and warmth. I dash inside to noise level that is over the top. It looks like a Las Vegas production going on, with people hurrying up and down the stairs, tables being unpacked and placed everywhere on the ground floor. The vendors for the tables also have the tablecloths, freshly washed and pressed hanging suspended on a rolling cart, as to not crease them. They swerve and dodge people to get at the end of the tables to start assembling the look for the event. My phone pings. It's the florist.

"Darci, we're running out of room to store all the decorations. These have to stay refrigerated or they'll wilt by Friday night."

"Let me see what we can do. I'll be over in a few minutes to look at the situation." I catch a breath and hurry out to my car. The phone pings again. "I'm getting in my car and on my way, Katy. Give me a few and I'll be there."

The phone is silent. I look down at the number. It's Brian.

"Oops, I'm sorry, Brian. I thought you were the florist."

"You sound busy."

"I really am. It's the life of the event planner!" I try to sound jovial.

"Look, Darci, I know things have been a mess. I'd like to get together and talk it over."

"I just can't, Brian. We both have a lot on our plates right now. I'm juggling things the best I can and well, I'm out of hands to juggle. Take care, Brian. I have to go." I disconnect and stare at my phone for a minute, only just now realizing I'm half in and half out of the car. I finish climbing in and start the engine. It rumbles and kicks in the heat. Biting my lip, I take one last look at the phone before dropping it in my purse. I hadn't planned for this conversation. It simply came out this way. As sad as it makes my heart feel, I still believe it's the best move for me and the children right now. I don't want to get involved with someone that still has their past on their shoulders.

By the time I make it to the florist, Katy has taken the initiative and rearranged her refrigeration units and is glowing with pride as I walk inside. "Wow. Look at all those flowers. You've done a splendid job getting everything organized and ready to go."

"Thanks, Darci. Sometimes you have to think outside the box and realize if you put in the effort, the reward is there waiting."

"I like that, Katy. I'm thrilled you came up with a solution. I would have had to ask the mayor to find us a remedy and that would be difficult at the last minute. I was already wondering how much room I had in my fridge at home!"

Katy laughs and covers her mouth with her hand.

"Since you have this all taken care of, I better run back to the hotel to see how things are going. The tables were being delivered while I was there earlier. It's crazy to think of this happening the day after tomorrow!"

"Good luck! I want to let you know you're doing a wonderful job with this. Everyone in town is looking forward to the Masquerade Ball. It's so exciting."

"Are you and Calvin attending?"

"We wouldn't miss it! It's been a long time since we've had the chance to go."

"I'll look forward to seeing you both there. Even as the planner, I know I'll enjoy all the magic of the night."

"What? No date for the big event?" Katy looks surprised.

"This really isn't a date event for an event planner. I have to be available to handle any little crisis that may arise, but it won't stop me from enjoying the festive event and watching all the wonderful couples showing up in their masks. We'll have a photographer there to capture the night. I'm excited just thinking of it."

"How early can I get started bringing the flowers on Friday?"

"I'm thinking around noon. That will give the other folks until then to get all the balloons suspended without worrying about knocking over flowers. If they finish earlier, I'll give you a call." Waving, I head out the door to double check on things back at the hotel.

I'm exhausted by the time I leave the hotel to pick up the kids at mom's house. It took me longer than expected. It's nearly three now. I get to the door and mom already has it open.

"I'm sorry, mom. I thought I'd be through long before now. It's amazing all the last-minute details that have to be attended to. Say, you're not looking too well."

"Your dad is worse. He went to bed at nine this morning. He has a slight fever and aching all over. I hate to say this, honey, especially with the party around the corner, but we better not watch the kids until we shake this stuff."

"I agree, mom. I'm so sorry you and dad have come down with this stuff. The flu, you think?"

"Most likely. If we feel better by Friday night…"

"Please, don't worry a bit. It's no problem at all. I'll find someone to watch them while I'm at the party."

"You might should start calling. An event like this, everyone will be going and most will need babysitters."

"I'll get right on it. Now, you should crawl into bed and rest, mom. I love you."

"Love you, too, sugar."

CHAPTER 26

I bundle the kids up in their jackets and get them buckled into the car seats before it really hits me. Mom's right. Everyone is planning on coming to this party and the chance of me finding a sitter will be difficult at best. Once home, the kids slide out of their coats and chase down the kittens. I don't know who is happiest to see them, the kittens or the kids!

I plop down at the kitchen table and pull out my address book, thumbing through the names to see if I can find someone to watch them Friday night. Shoot, I wish I had more notice. The event is the day after tomorrow. I'm sure others have lined up their sitters weeks in advance.

Three phone calls later, I still haven't found anyone. I'm just about to call another possibility when someone knocks at my door. I open it to find Rita standing there.

"Oh, hi, Rita. Come in out of that cold."

Rita comes in and walks to the kitchen table. "Have I caught you at a bad time?"

"It shows on my face?" I give her a slight frown. "Sorry. I'm just about ready to pull my hair out."

"What's wrong?"

"It's this Masquerade Ball Friday night. As the event organizer, I have to be there. Mom and dad had planned to watch Mattie and Ethan, but they aren't feeling well. Nothing terrible, maybe it's the flu bug. Anyway, I've been calling trying to line up a sitter and this late in the game, I haven't found anyone. What am I to do? I can't very well tug them to the Masquerade Ball and work too. Oh gosh, Rita, I'm so sorry. I didn't mean to just explode my problem to you. What did you come over for?"

Rita is silent for a moment, chewing on her lower lip. "I hadn't seen you in a few days and wanted to check on you. It's a good thing too."

"Why do you say that?"

"Because I think we can take care of your babysitter problems."

"We?"

"Uh, well, yes. Between the two of us, I think I have the answer."

"Well, don't keep me in suspense, I'm about to lose my hair over this."

"Hang on to your hair, Darci, I'll watch them for you."

"Oh my! Oh, Rita, do you mean it? I can't believe this. You are a saint. Are you sure you wouldn't rather be doing something else on New Year's Eve night?"

"It will be perfect. I was staying in anyway, watching the New Year's countdown like I do most years. This time I'll have company. If it's better for them, I'll come over here to watch them."

"I hope you're not allergic to cats! Mom and dad gave them kittens for Christmas. They are adorable and were rescued from the shopping center's parking lot."

"Are you kidding? Me allergic to animals? How could I be and still go to Brian's"

At the mention of his name, I drop my head and it goes silent again.

"I'm sorry, Darci. I didn't mean to bring his name up, it just kind of slipped out."

"No, it's fine. I can't expect you to stop mentioning your brother just because—things are different right now."

"It doesn't have to be this way, Darci." She looks at me with velvety brown eyes.

"I really appreciate your offer to watch the kids for me Friday night, I mean that. You're a dear to do so, but Rita, I've got to get passed all this drama with Samantha. To do so, I need some distance from Brian as he deals with what's on his plate."

"I'm sure if you talked with him, you'd find out all he wants on his plate is you."

I feel a tear burn the corner of my eye. "That's a sweet thing to say, but I know differently. I told him when he called today that I don't have time for him or the drama. I'm sorry, Rita. Don't let this be a wedge between us. I'm going to need a friend more than ever, right now."

She solemnly nods her head, holding back any words she would like to say.

"What time would you like me to come over Friday?"

"Could you make it by six p.m.? I'll have to get to the hotel early in order to take care of the last-minute details and be there for the first arrivals, which should be the mayor and his wife and their group."

"That will be fine with me," Rita says, smiling.

"I'll order in pizza for everyone. How does that sound?"

"Delicious. I love pizza." She smiles.

"Thank you so much. You don't know how much easier you just made it for me."

"Me, too," she says. I look puzzled until she explains. "Now, I get to have company, pizza, and ring in the New Year's the way I want to."

"You're such a good sport. I'll see you Friday!"

She turns to hug me, giggles, and trots of to her apartment. Sometimes I think she may be my guardian angel. She's always there when I desperately need help. I mumble to myself, *She sure is happy just to be babysitting.*

Over a bowl of chicken and dumplings at dinner, I let Mattie and Ethan know Rita will be watching them on New Year's Eve right here at home. They are a little sad not to be going to Grandma and Grandpa's house for New Year's, but they understand and like that they will be home with their kitties. Gone are those shy little balls of fur, and here are the confident, springy kittens ready for play. I silently thank my dad for taking them home and thinking to give them to my children. It was the best decision ever. For me, it's even better than the ponies because they can be with them every day.

After their baths, they're in their fuzzy jammies and the kittens are curled up in their beds, right next to the children's beds. They don't stay there long, every time I peek in on the children during the night, the kittens have crawled up onto the beds and next to their person. I allow it. They seem to know when to dodge a rolling arm or a leg when the children move about at night. Reading them a story helps us all unwind from the day and gives good thoughts for dreams.

I slip into my room and look in the closet. I pull out the gown I plan on wearing to the Ball. It's a simple gown: long, black velvet with an illusion neckline and black lace sleeves with gold at the bottom of the lace sleeves. I think something with classic lines could be worn to many different occasions, or so I told myself when I purchased it. Instead of heels, I opt for black wedges of about two inches. Even though the entrance will be de-iced and a carpet laid down, it still could mean slippery walking from my car to the entrance. That makes me envious of the couples attending. They'll at least have someone who will drop them off at the entrance. I look at my mask again. A shot of electricity moves through me. It's so magical, I can almost find myself in a fairytale or even one of those specially made for television Christmas stories. It's enough to make me glide around the room with the gown in my hand. I grin at myself for being so caught up in the moment, but moments are what make a lifetime and I want to cherish all the moments I have.

When I rise in the morning, I make my list of call backs to make sure I have all things in order for Friday. Today will be busy and hectic, but fortunately I should be able to handle most of it from home. We didn't get any more snow and ice last night, so if I have to get out and about, I'll just bundle up Mattie and Ethan and bring them with me.

In the midst of making twenty some odd phone calls, I have to wait for call backs. This is the most frustrating part of the job. All could be well and fine, but until I get that call that says it is, my heart palpitates in worry. It plays havoc on a good manicure, too. I glance at my nails before I'm tempted to chew on them. I have to call back the hotel to see if the people doing the balloon drop can set up this afternoon, instead of on Friday. Someone's signal got crossed and one of the helpers can't make it in to Hope Falls on Friday. I slap my palm against my forehead wondering what else is going to throw me a curve ball. The phone rings and I answer it cautiously.

"Hello?"

"Well, I hope your satisfied little-miss-going-to-have-it-my-way."

"Samantha?" I look down at the number, but it's different than last time. I feel my eyes widen in disbelief. "Why are you calling me? I have nothing to say to you."

"I'm sure you don't, not now, not after you got everything you wanted!"

"What's that supposed to mean?"

"As if you didn't know! Don't try to play that game with me. I invented it!"

"Samantha, I assure you I haven't a clue to what you are talking about. Have you been into the alcohol?"

"It's not likely I'd get any around here, that's for sure."

"Look. Does Brian know you're on the phone?"

"Stop playing all coy. You know darn well Brian doesn't give a crap what I do or where I'm doing it."

"You're not making sense to me. Whatever you're mad at, you can leave me out of it. I told Brian I'm done with his drama.

You can kindly stop calling me." I'm ready to end the call when I hear a surprised, *"You what?"*

"So, he didn't fill you in?" Samantha stutters.

"Fill me in with what, Samantha. I'm one second away from hanging up on you. I have tons of work to get done. Yes, there are still females that work." Okay, I admit it. I could have passed on saying that last part, but she's getting under my skin.

"Hang up if you want to, then you'll never learn why I'm so surprised by everything you're saying."

"What I'm saying? All you are doing is talking in some kind of twisted riddles. I can't make any sense as to what you're saying or why you're calling *me*."

"Brian threw us out, that's what."

I gasp. "He what?"

"You heard me. He threw us out and right before New Year's. What kind of man can do that to a woman he loved and who's all banged up?" She's crying. Oh, lordie, no. Not the crying.

"Surely you don't mean that. Where are you?"

"Oh, not out in the cold. No. He made this grand gesture telling me and Billy he had an amazing surprise for us. Well, of course, I was excited and so was Billy. We couldn't imagine what he had planned especially after—Christmas night. I thought, that's just like a man, he says one thing, but means another. I don't have to tell you my hopes were sky high. And then, he pulls up in front of this quaint Victorian house or something. I thought it may be a bed and breakfast. I've never known Brian to go in for that sort of thing but being the holidays and all…" She pauses. "But it wasn't a bed and breakfast place. It's a medical building! They call it…"

"*The Therapy House*. I've heard of it." I'm trying to keep the smile from my voice. He did it, he actually did it! He took her and Billy to a place that will help her until the casts can be removed and now he doesn't have to play nursemaid to her any longer.

"Well, I've never been thrown to the curb like this before."

"From what I understand, *The Therapy House* is state of the art. You have private rooms and 24 hour-a-day help. I can't imagine it's very inexpensive."

"I wouldn't know. I guess he can clean his conscious by footing the bill at this place. It's nothing like being at home and having all your things around you."

"I'm sure your mother will come to visit and bring you whatever you want."

"That's not the point. The point is whatever you told Brian made him do this to me, to us. Poor Billy. Did he even think of how hard it will be for Billy?"

"I'm sure if Billy isn't there with you, he can go to your mom's. He'd probably be a great help to her with her working all those hours."

"Well, I hope you're happy. You ruined Christmas and now New Year's. One of these days Brian is going to wake up and see what type of woman you are and what he left behind in me."

"Samantha, dear. I think he already has." I end the call.

I add that number to the list of blocked numbers from Samantha. I feel like I just was dropped off by a tornado. I wish I would have recorded the call. Everything she said is a blur now. I spent far too much time trying to interpret what she meant to hear what she was saying. Brian took her to *The Therapy House*. I'm speechless. I know my dad told Brian about the place, but really? I would never have guessed he would be bold enough to load them in the truck and take them over there. Bravo to you, Brian. This puts a new twist on things, or it would have, if I hadn't already told Brian to leave me be. Maybe after this New Year's gala is over, we can make time to talk and see where it goes. I'm not going to get my hopes up. After all, I did tell him I didn't want to be a part of all this drama. Thankfully, I still have lots of work to keep me busy and then tomorrow is the big event. No time for wishing I hadn't said this or that. It is what it is.

I must say the rest of my phone calls are jubilant. For once, speaking to Samantha didn't throw a dark cloak over me, weighing me down. I could go on to say I feel as light as a feather. It's really put the festive back into the festivities for me and I can't wait for the Ball tomorrow. I'll be swaying to the music all night and dreaming of what the future holds.

CHAPTER 27

Checking the clock in the kitchen, I decide to give mom a call to see how they are feeling and to let her know what I learned from Samantha today. That ought to give her and dad something to think about as they get better.

"Hello, mom. How are you and day doing today?"

"Hi, honey. We're surviving is about it. We're coughing so much our ribs feel kicked."

"Oh, no. Have you made a call into the doctor?"

"Not just yet. You know your father. He wants to see if we can shake it, first. I do think we're over the hump, though. I'm sorry, this is such rotten timing."

"Don't worry, mom. You just get better. I've got some great news to share."

"I could use some of that. What's new?"

"The first thing is I've lined up a sitter for tomorrow night. Rita, from next door, volunteered. That will be wonderful as she will come over here and the kids don't have to go anywhere."

"That's wonderful. Didn't you mention Rita is Brian's sister?"

"Yes, I did. Here's the even bigger news. Samantha called me again."

"She what? That little meddling minx!"

"Calm down, mom. Listen. She was upset when she called and it took me forever to figure out why. You won't believe this, but Brian took them and left them at *The Therapy House*! Tell dad that him mentioning it certainly gave Brian an option he didn't think he had."

"Have you talked to him, yet?"

"Brian? Well, not really. This all happened just today and I'm still trying to get everything set up for the Ball tomorrow. Anyway, see… Brian called me yesterday and wanted to get together to talk about this mess. I told him no. I had too much on my plate and didn't have time for the drama."

"Darci…"

"I know, mom. I just had had it with all of the Samantha stuff. Anyway, I've got to concentrate on getting this event pulled together and then I'll call him. Even though he did move Samantha and Billy out, I'm still bothered that he finds it necessary to cater to them at Samantha's slightest whim."

"It seems to me Brian has found a way to put that passed him. Maybe it's time you do so, too?"

I chuckle. "Point taken, mom. Do you need me too run you by any food or some takeout?"

"No, we're fine. I made a crock pot full of chicken soup. I do swear it's what is making us sleep better. Do me a favor. Since you won't be dropping the kids off tomorrow. Take one of those selfies when you're all decked out. I want to see your dress and mask."

"I will, I promise. I'm getting so excited! I haven't been to a masquerade party since I was little and you and dad had one at our house one year."

"Oh, that was so much fun. I really wish we felt better and could attend. Maybe next year."

"Let's see if this year goes off without many problems, first. They may can me and hire a new event coordinator."

"Not on your life. You've done fabulous at the job and don't you think otherwise."

"Thanks, mom. Well, I better get some food for the kiddos. I'll talk to you soon. Bye."

"Bye, honey."

After looking at the available options, I whip up a steaming pot of spaghetti. It's one of our favorites, and with garlic toast and salad it's sheer perfection. After dinner is done and dishes washed, it's bath time for the kids and then a snuggle and bedtime story. I look forward to the ending of the day when we can finally take a deep breath and unwind. There's nothing better than snuggling up with your kids and reading. I have a feeling when I'm old and grey, I'll still remember these precious moments. That's why I don't want to miss a single evening of this relaxing bliss.

It doesn't take long for them to nod off to sleep. I sit here a little longer listening to them breathing. Their little faces are like sleeping angels. It's hard to catch them so still during the day. I cover each of them up to their chins and turn off the light. The lamps on their nightstands cast a warm glow across the room. As soon as I leave the rocking chair, Dancer leaves her bed and jumps up to snuggle with Mattie. It's as lovely as any picture.

Waking up, I turn on the news to catch the daily forecast. Perfect, no storm in sight. That's a load off my mind. A storm could mean low attendance, or just as bad, a mess at dropping off the ladies to enter the hotel. Who wants to track through slush to get to the hotel's entrance? I sigh a huge relief. Now I just need to make sure all the deliveries, the caterers, and the rest of it is going on as planned. Chewing on my lip, I wonder whether I should ask Rita is she could watch Mattie and Ethan for a few hours while I check at the hotel to make sure everything is on schedule, or if I should bundle them up and take them with me? I decide to take a shower and play phone tag for a bit. Maybe I won't need to go prior to tonight. I'll keep my fingers crossed.

The shower is heavenly. I use my favorite shampoo infused with vanilla and honey. It leaves a pleasant after-scent that lingers and I don't feel the need of any heavy perfume. I comb out my curls and lightly towel-dry my hair. For tonight, I'll leave my hair down. I'm tempted to grab the mask and try it on, just for the fun of it. I grin at myself in the mirror, for I haven't felt this much like a kid in a long while. Even though I'll be working at the event it doesn't do anything to dampen my mood. I can't wait to see all our townspeople come out tonight, dressed to the hilt and having a great New Year's Eve.

I dress in jeans and a sweater and look in on the kids. They are still sleeping. Time to make them some oatmeal and toast to keep those bellies warm and full. While I'm getting breakfast on the table, Katy calls from the florist.

"I wanted to let you know I've already been to the hotel. The vendors providing the balloon drop for midnight have already been there and it's all set up. I didn't know that many of our businesses gave away coupons to put in the balloon or I would have donated some, myself."

"I'm sorry, Katy. It was a last-minute idea that one of the ladies at *The Gift and Gab* suggested. We had several donate at the last minute to make the balloon drop more fun. Now people will have to be trying to bust open balloons for prizes. I hope we get to do this event again because I'm learning so much to make the next one even better than ever."

"I can tell you, everyone and I mean everyone is looking forward to tonight. You wouldn't believe the amount of people who already stopped in the hotel to take a peek. The Wilhelms have had to close off the areas with the tables so they won't get messed up before tonight. I even saw the photographer of our newspaper down there taking pictures for the *before* look. This event is going to go down in the history books, I just know it."

"I'm thrilled you think so. I'm starting to get nervous. I want everything to be perfect."

"It will be, you wait and see. The reason I called is I wanted to get an early start at bringing all the flowers out. Since we'll be attending the party, I'd like to get home in plenty of time to shower and look my best for the evening."

"Of course. Go on out. The only delay I was thinking of was the balloon drop people, but since they've already been there and completed their task, you are free to load up and bring it all to the hotel. Were you able to distinguish where the mayor and his wife and their friends will be sitting? That's the table we want to have the large swag of flowers on."

"Yes, no problem. It even has a reserved sign on it for the mayor and his party. I've got this. Don't worry. Everyone is getting their parts done without any problems. If I hear of see anything you should know about while I'm delivering the flowers, I'll give you a head's up, how's that sound?"

"It sounds lovely. I really should be out there but with the children home, it presents a bit of a problem. Not one I can't handle if need be, mind you, it just makes it easier if I don't have to run to town."

"Like I said, I'll let you know of anything I see needing your help."

"Thanks, Katy. I appreciate you. If I don't see you before, I'll see you at the event."

"Yes you will. I can't wait for us to show you our masks. You'll love them!"

"I can't wait, either. Bye for now."

Chapter 28

Mattie comes into the kitchen rubbing the sleep from her eyes. "I'm hungry."

"Good, go get your brother while I set the table, would you?"

"Yes, mommy."

Breakfast is devoured in nothing flat and I help Ethan get into his jeans, sweater, and boots. They want to play outside today while the sun is shining. I open the patio door so they can go out to the backyard. At least I refer to it as a backyard, it's mostly a patio with a two-lawnmower pass patch of grass. But, from all the apartments we looked at, these were the only ones that had that touch of "home."

While the kiddos are playing outside, it leaves me time to finish my calls. I get worried when I call the hotel line and no one answers. I redial two more times. Once, it rang and rang and the last time it went immediately to a busy signal. I'm twisting my hands together. It's not like the Wilhelms to not answer. I try again. This time a breathless Margery Wilhelm answers, "The Scarlet Leaf, how may I help you?"

"Hello, Mrs. Wilhelm. This is Darci."

"Goodness, child. This place is running full steam ahead."

"Is everything okay?"

"Okay? We haven't had this many people in the hotel for decades! To say we got caught off-guard is an understatement.

We'll be okay now that I've called my grandnieces to come lend a hand. I just finished showing them how to set a room for our guests. Can you imagine, we only have four rooms vacant? Not only have people bought tickets to the Masquerade Ball, but most have snuck in to take a look. Loving what they saw, they immediately booked rooms! I haven't been this tuckered in a long while."

"I'm sorry for any inconvenience this has caused you and the hotel. I'll be there in a dash to help out."

"You misunderstand. We are grateful; indeed, we are thrilled to have this much support. Most of the guests are from right here in Hope Falls. They could easily attend the function and return home, but they've chosen to stay with us. It a great honor to have them here and their support. Dear, the one thing most folks don't know is we have been running the hotel out of love and our own pocketbooks. It hasn't shown a profit in years, but since we're the fourth generation to run the hotel, we just couldn't close its doors. There is too much history in these walls."

"I had no idea, Mrs. Wilhelm! I have a feeling your pocketbook running days will cease once everyone gets a taste of your hotel. I certainly will put the word out about *The Scarlet Leaf*, letting people know it's a destination unto itself."

"You are a dear. We've had to let go so many who had worked here for years. I have a call in to see if some will return to make this the best event ever. Don't worry on the hotel end, we won't let you down."

"I'm not the least bit worried about the hotel, but I am very anxious to see things in full-throttle. I will come down as soon as I can manage to make sure everything for the Ball is ready to go."

"We'll see you then. Or, I should hope to, the way the guests are flooding in, I can't be certain."

"That is quite alright. This phone call has excited me to no end. Bye, Mrs. Wilhelm."

"Goodbye, Darci."

Sitting at the table, a smile spreads across my face. I would have never known the Wilhelms were keeping the hotel open out of their loyalty and love of the place. It makes me warm inside to think this event is driving guests to stay at the hotel, when as Mrs. Wilhelm mentioned, there really wasn't a need to do so. I know when I get to the hotel, there probably won't be any fires I need to put out, but to hear Katy and now, Mrs. Wilhelm speak of the hotel, I'm dying to take a look myself. It feels like magic is coursing through our town and I don't want to miss it.

Fortunately, Mattie and Ethan are still presentable so I tell them I'm taking them with me to see how the hotel is decorated. They are as excited as I am, and that's a lot of excitement. We make it out to the car and I get them ready to go. Climbing into the car, I'm shocked to hear a fire truck race by. My eyes grow with alarm. It's headed downtown. My first thought is *the hotel!*

I'm not exactly following the fire truck, but headed in the same direction. Ethan can't stop talking about it and it sets my nerves on edge. What are we going to do if it's the hotel? My heart races. I don't see smoke yet. Biting my lip, I make the turn where the hotel comes into clear view. Oh! Thank goodness, the fire truck has passed it. Looking at my hands, they are in a white-knuckled death grip on the steering wheel. Mercy, I need a cup of coffee in the worst way.

I park and take in the sight. The parking lot already has several cars and trucks as well as the caterers' vehicle unloading stacks of plates, utensils, and warmers. Out front, the evergreen topiaries have been dressed in silver and gold streamers with stars shooting out of the greenery. The entrance with their glass-encased oak doors gleam with welcome. Mattie and Ethan are full of ohhs and ahhs. They even have a door man standing at the entrance. He looks dashing in long, woolen double-breasted black coat, black pants with a gold stripe running down the outside of the legs, and a cap matching the coat. Completely elegant. He is gesturing to two men how to lay the carpet on the inside of the hotel doors and the large runner on the outside. We stand still and watch as they add their touch. It's a crimson runner that greets the guests at the curbside, continuing to the double front doors of the hotel.

I guide the children onto the carpet and we follow it to the hotel doors. The door man opens the door for us, exchanging pleasantries. On the inside, we step onto a plush carpet looking like a sky full of stars. It's exquisite. We don't know what to take in first, there are so many lovely decorations absolutely everywhere the eyes land. I take Mattie and Ethan by their hands and guide them to where the tables are set behind two swinging wooden doors. I open a door and my breath is taken away. Fairy lights glisten from overhead and the tables are set with alternating silver and black to gold and black with swags of netting laced with lights and stars swirling around vases of roses. It is stunning.

"It's a fairy tale place, Mommy." Ethan gushes with Mattie nodding in complete agreement.

"I want pictures, Mommy. Will you take some?" Mattie asks.

"Yes, and if you won't touch the decorations, I'll take one right now with you standing in front of the tables."

"Oh, yes!" They hold hands and stand in front of the closest table as I dig out my phone to take several pictures. They look so good, I think I'll print these out and give mom and dad a few.

I escort them out of the room to hear part of the conversation Mrs. Wilhelm is having.

"Oh my! Well, yes. I'll get two rooms ready. That won't be necessary, Mira. We'll take care of it."

I walk up right as she hangs up the phone, shaking her head.

"What is it, Mrs. Wilhelm?"

"There's been a fire," she says, still dismayed.

"I forgot all about it. We followed a fire truck on our way here. I was so relieved it wasn't the hotel, it just went out of my thoughts. Where was the fire? Was it bad?"

"Over at *The Therapy House*. It didn't cause a lot of damage, but the smoke is thick. They need their guests to stay somewhere else overnight."

Suddenly, I feel like I swallowed a ten-pound bowling ball. "You are giving them rooms, here?"

"It's the very least we can do. They have one gentleman recovering from a stroke and a lady with both arms broken. How terrible it must be for them."

"What happened?"

"The fire department is still investigating, but it looks like the culprit was a candle unattended. That seems to be the source of many fires, particularly this time of year. It's a good thing we have all the rooms ready. They'll be bringing them over soon."

"Such awful timing, and here the hotel will be much louder than it normally is. I hope the rooms you have will be far away from the event."

"I hadn't thought of that, but yes, I have just the thing. The rooms will be on the backside of the hotel where the noise level should be at a minimum. Thank you for that reminder, dear."

"Everything looks lovely. I'm off to get the children home and get ready for the evening, myself. I'll see you later."

I wave goodbye as we head back to the car. How is it that Samantha turns up every time I turn around? A fire at *The Therapy House*? No doubt it started in her room. Just when I believe I can get past thinking about her, here she is again. If I didn't know better, I'd swear she learned of tonight's festivities and wanted to make darn sure she was included, invitation or not. I could just scream. I don't have time for any of her drama and everywhere she goes, there's drama.

Once home, I put on a pot of coffee to settle my nerves. Almost lunch time, I open up a few cans of stew to go with the cornbread I have leftover. That should be filling for all of us and I don't know if I'll even have time to eat tonight. Having not done this event before, I need to be on my toes to handle anything that comes my way so eating may be taking a few nibbles here and there.

After lunch, the kids curl up for a nap and I think that is the best idea of the day. I grab my thick, soft blanket at the foot of my bed, slip off my shoes, and pull a pillow from under the bedspread and melt into it. If I can bank in a few hours of sleeping, maybe I won't yawn the night away. That would be embarrassing; the event coordinator looking bored at the event she put together. I hope I can shush my mind long enough to fall asleep.

CHAPTER 29

I stretch and wiggle my toes under my blanket. Rolling my head to the side, I look at the alarm clock. Oh my goodness! It's almost three-thirty. I can't believe I slept this long. I can't believe the *kids* slept this long. Jumping up, I check their room and they are out of bed. I find them in the living room. Ethan is on the floor wallowing with his kitten and Mattie is on the couch. They have cartoons on, but at a low volume.

"Hi, Mommy. You're awake," Mattie says.

"Have you two been awake long?"

"Not really. We've watched one cartoon" Mattie replies.

"I'll get you some juice and fruit, does that sound good?"

"Yes, please."

I make a plate for each of them with grapes and cut up apples. I open the top of vanilla yogurt and place a big dallop on each of their plates to dip their apples into. I pour each a glass of orange juice. That ought to tie them over until the pizza arrives. Making a mental note to call the pizzeria at five, I sit and chat with them as they enjoy their snack. My thoughts return to the fire and Samantha. What am I going to do if she shows up at the party? As I have a chance to think it over, it's highly unlikely since this is a last-minute change of address for her and I'm sure she hasn't had time or even the funds to go out and buy something for tonight. I can only keep my fingers crossed and my eyes open. My eyes spring wide as I think, *Masquerade*... She could show up and I may not even recognize her. My jaw drops.

"Mommy? You're making funny faces," Mattie notes.

"I am? I was thinking of so many things at once. Sometimes mommies make those faces when their brains get too full."

"Then I bet I make those faces a lot in school. My brain always feels like there is too much in there."

I have to laugh. From the words of children, so goes life. Cleaning up their snack plates, I let them return to the cartoons and I head to my bedroom to lay out my ensemble. It's still two hours before I need to leave, but I want so much to dress now. Biting my lip I study the dress, purse, shoes, and mask. With two loose children in the house, it's better to wait until right before I leave to get dressed. I know the mask will conceal my face until dinner, but I still need to wear make-up for when the mask comes off. Plus, we re-mask before the balloon drop. That will make it all that much more fun to watch people chasing balloons to pop and look for prizes. Sitting down at my vanity, I brush out my hair and slide open the drawer to retrieve my make-up. The first thing I notice is the silver necklace with the tiny reindeer. I sigh deeply.

If it hadn't have been for this recent episode with the fire and Samantha now at the hotel, I could have dreamed of Brian showing up and being with me at the event. I'm sure that's the last thing on his mind after I cut him off on the phone call the other day. Even if there still is a chance to call him before the party, I can't bring myself to do it knowing Samantha will be on premise. It's like she has this hidden antenna that go up anytime Brian and I are in the same vicinity. I know even after Brian dropped her off at *The Therapy House*, it won't stop her from trying to get back with him. Running the chain through my hands I decide to wear the necklace. It's sort of a good luck charm to me for all the fun we were able to have with Brian and his family. I shrug. Who knows. It may be over with, or it may not be, but the charming necklace will keep my hope alive, at least for tonight. As pragmatic as I am on some things, other times I'm a hopeless romantic. Digging through my jewelry I find a sweet pair of earrings to wear. They look like shooting stars and spin while I'm wearing them. The nice thing about them is the stars are both silver and gold so it matches my necklace color and the gold in my gown. Since my hair has a natural curl to it, I save time not having to use rollers or a curling iron.

I still have over an hour and a half to go before leaving. I call mom and give her an update.

"Hi, mom. How are you and dad?"

"Hello, Darci. We are on the mend. We tire quickly, but we're able to stay out of bed all day now. The coughing and sneezing has come to a stop, thank goodness. My nose was starting to look like Rudolf!" She chuckles good naturedly and it puts my mind at ease.

"Did you hear the fire truck earlier?" I ask.

"Yes, we did. We wondered what was going on. It sounded off in the distance."

You aren't going to believe this. It went to *The Therapy House*."

"No! Oh gracious, was anyone hurt?"

"It's okay, mom. Most of the damage seems to be just from smoke. But um, this is where Samantha is, or I mean, was." I hear mom catch her breath.

"Spill the beans. You know more than you're saying."

"I was getting to it. They only had an older man there recovering from a stroke and Samantha and her son. They had to find them temporary quarters for the evening as they get rid of the smoke and any damage. They will have a free room at the hotel."

The telephone goes quiet.

"Mom? Are you there?"

"I am, I just can't believe what I just heard. Samantha... there at the Masquerade party?"

"Well, realistically, maybe not at the event, but just knowing she's going to be at the hotel on the night of my big event is enough to get my heart racing. I can never guess what she will do next."

"Don't let her ruin your night. Besides, she's in casts on both arms. It's not like she can get all gussied up and go to the event."

"True. I'll keep my eyes open for a two-cast woman sneaking in."

"That's my girl. You'll be the belle at the ball and will hear accolades from everyone. I know this was hard to put together, but the hard part is done now. You need to relax, unwind and enjoy tonight. Don't forget to take a picture for us."

"Thanks, mom. I always feel better after talking to you."

"Aw, any time, my love. Off you go. Go get yourself ready for the party.

"Bye, mom." I sit there smiling. She can always get me to smile when I'm starting to get a panic attack. She's right. Tonight will be a night for no worries. Time to ring in the New Year full of hope and possibilities.

After getting Mattie and Ethan bathed and in their sleepers, I remind them to be good when Rita comes over and not to constantly try to put the kittens in her lap. Mattie laughs, but nods.

"She's used to animals because Brian is her brother," she retorts, as if I've forgotten.

"She's used to the *farm* animals, we don't know about kittens."

"If she loves animals, she loves all animals, silly."

Just what I need, a precocious child. "At least you can ask her when she gets here, okay?"

"Yes, Mommy."

I ruffle her hair and retreat to my bedroom to get ready. When I slip on the gown, it feels as if I'm stepping into a different time. It's a bit long without my shoes on, but it fits well. I spin a bit to watch the sleeves move in the air. The dress is a sheath style, so it hardly moves from my body. Now, the fun part. Turning to go into the closet, I remove the box with the mask. Returning to the vanity, I carefully slip it over my hair. The effect makes me catch my breath. There's a new person staring at me from the mirror. The mask with its ivory face and eyelids painted a golden shimmering color has white appliqued lace around one eye that travels in splendid tendrils down the cheek, leaving the other half of the mask with the black and gold half of a butterfly wing accented with oblong pearls. It's exquisite and it's perfect for the gown I'm wearing. I slip on my shoes so I can show the children what I will look like at the ball.

Opening the bedroom door, I call them to me. "Mattie. Ethan. Come see my outfit for the Masquerade Ball."

They come running and stop suddenly at my door, eyes wide and mouths open.

"It's okay, it's Mommy."

Mattie shakes her head no, her eyes growing wider still. "You look like a fairy princess!"

I wish they could see my smile underneath the mask. I feel like a princess tonight. I removed the mask and they grin. "I can't very well wear the mask until I get to the hotel, otherwise I might not see as well when I'm driving."

"Don't forget to take a picture for Grandma and Grandpa, or they'll be mad," Mattie reminds me.

"When Rita gets here, I'll have her take one for me." Just as I utter the words, the doorbell rings. "I bet that's Rita."

I answer the door to have Rita take a step back, looking at my dress.

"You look beautiful, Darci, but then you always do, no matter what you're wearing," Rita says.

"You're so kind. Come in, come in. Would you do me a favor? My parents want a picture of me in my gown and mask. If you take the picture, you'll be able to capture the whole thing better than if I try to take a selfie picture."

"I'll be happy to."

"Just a second, I need to go put my mask back on. I'll be right back." I return to the bedroom and sit at the vanity, sliding the mask back over my curls. When I'm satisfied I have it straight, I go back to the living room. Rita stares at me almost the same way the children did. She utters one word.

"Magical."

"Thank you! I feel transformed into a beautiful swan."

"Here, go stand by the wall so I can get the complete picture." She takes my phone and gets it ready to take the picture. "I'm going to take a few to make sure you have what you want for your parents." As she clicks away, I know my eyes are sparkling because I'm grinning so big under the mask.

"One second, Darci. I want to take one with my phone, if you don't mind."

"No, that's fine." Now I'm starting to feel as if I'm walking the red carpet somewhere. It's a heavenly feeling. She takes one or two pictures, then I remove the mask and grab my clutch from the bedroom.

"I've called in the pizza order and they said they're running a bit longer than normal. They should be here in about forty-five minutes. It's already paid for, as well as the drinks. I hope you'll have a fun evening together. I appreciate you so much for watching Mattie and Ethan."

"I'm happy to be spending the evening with them. We'll have great fun, guaranteed."

I kiss the children and give Rita a big hug before heading to the door.

"You go have the night of a lifetime. I can't wait to hear all about it when you come home." Her eyes dance as if she, too, were going to the ball.

"Goodbye and Happy New Year!" I say as my hand reaches for the doorknob.

"Oh! I about forgot. I have a bag of party favors and horns I left just inside my door. We'll use those to ring in the New Year." She dodges past me and unlocks her door to grab the bag of party favors. I shake my head. She thinks of everything.

"Now, off you go to the Ball. You don't want to be late, do you?"

"As it is, I'm arriving much earlier than most of the guests will be there."

"I doubt that, not with all the cars already parked in the parking lot."

"You know, I forgot about that. Mrs. Wilhelm said the hotel is booked so that means many of those attending the Ball are already at the hotel! Instead of arriving early, now I feel like I'm running late."

"It will be fine. Just do your best to have a grand time tonight. There's something about the New Year that makes all things more magical than any other day. And you in that gown and mask! I'll not wonder if some Prince Charming comes and runs away with you!"

I laugh and swish my hand dismissively. She knows the only one I've had eyes for is her brother. The timing is just wrong for us this year… But who's to say *next* year won't be better? I step out into the night. It's true. It does feel magical. My heart speeds up and I have the hardest time not smiling. Not a person is in the parking lot as I step towards my car and yet, it feels like eyes are watching me. I self-consciously shake my head at my silliness. Even so, this one time, it makes me feel as if the night is for only me. It's amazing what a mask can do.

CHAPTER 30

The drive is short and as I round the bend and see the hotel, I gasp. It is stunning with the streamers and twinkling lights around the entrance. Rita is right, the parking lot is already near full, but I've lucked out with a spot close to the hotel. Perhaps my 'fairy godmother' arranged it for me. I grin pulling down my visor, I turn the light on to illuminate the mirror so I can slip the mask on. Once on, I slip out of the car and as my steps take me further away, I start feeling as if I'm someone else. Someone who isn't just a divorcee or a single mother, someone who is mysterious… someone who for once in her life gets to live large.

The doorman steps down the stair and offers his arm to guide me through the door. "May I say you look beautiful this night. I hope your better half knows how lucky he is." I want to giggle. He has no idea who I am! I play into his words and nod slightly as I enter through the main doors.

The hotel has been transformed into a stunning land of enchantment. I can't believe it's the same place I was at yesterday. Swags of greenery with twinkling lights and ribbons draped around them hang over the area entering the bar, and the double doors across the way are now open with a matching swag over the doorway. Candles shimmer on the tables, lighting up the floral arrangements. New Year's hats perch on the seats for the partygoers and horns and whistles sit on the tables. I'm close to tears as I take in the beauty of it all.

I turn away from it and go to the hotel's check-in desk. Mr. and Mrs. Wilhelm are dressed in black and smiling up a storm as they give a set of keys to a couple not yet in their masks and dress wear. I stand silently behind the couple and move to the desk as they move away.

"Well, hello, lovely lady. What can we do for you?" Mr. Wilhelm says extravagantly, as he bends at mid-waist.

I slip off my mask to hear them both give a surprised gasp. "Hello. I thought I'd arrive early in case there are any last-minute problems."

"Why, I never would have guessed that was you, Darci! Not that you aren't always lovely," Mrs. Wilhelm says, graciously.

"Thank you. I do feel rather different all dressed up and with the mask. It's absolutely exciting, like playing dress up as a child."

"I told Margery the same thing a bit ago. There's no reason for us to wait to wear our masks. It's practically mandatory to look the part, wouldn't you agree?"

"I think that's a fabulous idea. It makes it more exciting as we go through the evening."

Mr. Wilhelm smiles and reaches under the counter to retrieve his mask. It has a very 'phantom of the opera' look to it and looks perfect on him. Mrs. Wilhelm slides her out as well. I dare say it catches me off guard. It has a black and silver half mask with plumes of feathers on the left side. When she slips it on, she is someone different altogether. Perhaps someone from the flapper days. Regal, yet flirty, too. We chat for a few minutes before I decide to check in on the tables. I see guests coming down the stairs and taking seats.

Laughing guests chatter from table to table. It's terribly early, yet several tables have guests sitting at them. I make a point to stop to visit with each table. It seems the Wilhelms are doing double-duty by collecting the tickets for tonight's event.

Instead of name tags given to those with tickets, they have their hands stamped with the hotel's own stamp, showing the scarlet leaf, the hotel's name. I think it's a nice touch and lets me know as I greet the festive party goers whether they have purchased a ticket without the embarrassment of asking them.

Introducing myself, as the event organizer and my name, I'm pleased to hear them gush about the setup for the evening. In our small community most have, in the recent past, had to go to the larger cities to revel in the New Year, and by us offering this event they are thrilled to not make the drive with so many people hurrying to get to their destinations. We are more than happy to have them stay in our town and support our local businesses. As I think of those who contributed gift coupons for the balloon drop, I learned that each business reaps far more than they donate because of bringing a friend or spouse along as they redeem them, plus they gain returning customers if they are happy with their items.

I find myself concerned at the early turnout. The caterers won't have the meals ready until shortly after eight p.m. and there isn't much for the early birds to do except have drinks from the bar. So far, only six tables have guests at them so perhaps all will go well. Making my way back to the check-in desk, I see a string of attendees lining up to turn in their tickets. I hurry over to see if I can help. By asking the people how many are staying at the hotel and how many are just attending the event, I can break them into separate lines. I borrow a stamp and pad from the Wilhelms and collect the tickets from those who are only attending the Masquerade Ball. I can see it relieves the pressure on the Wilhelms, who can now get about their normal business, and it allows me time to get to know some of the people attending. I'll never remember all of their names, but the time visiting with them keeps a smile on my face.

I'm shocked when I turn to see Gretchen from the *Kountry Kitchen* walking into the room with her arms stacked with baskets. She's puffing a long strand of red hair out of her eyes.

"Gretchen? What can I help you with?"

"It would be grand if you would hold half of these baskets," she replies, out of breath. "Jacob will bring in the others when he arrives. I didn't have enough room in my car to bring them all."

"Of course. What are you doing with them?" I'm still at a loss why she's entering the ball room with country baskets.

"Mayor Henshaw called last night and asked if I could fulfill a request. He stated how the hotel is booked-up and the Ball wasn't due to start until eight p.m. His concern was not having food for those who are coming early to the party. The hotel has been caught a bit off-guard with all those that have booked rooms and their own kitchen is cooking non-stop to meet the needs of the hotel guests. These small baskets will provide those at tables something to nibble on until their dinner arrives. I have cheese wedges, crackers, grape bunches plus our own mini muffins."

"How wonderful and a great forethought by our Mayor. We so appreciate you working extra hard to provide these for the guests." I don't say it, but I'm wondering how much this extra will cost because our budget for the event has already been spent. It's almost like she's reading my mind when she replies.

"Now, I can rush back to the house and change for the party! The Mayor is paying for our sitter and our tickets for the evening as well as purchasing two gift certificates for two hundred dollars each for a drawing tonight." Her smile is infectious. I return the same to her as she rushes back out of the ballroom.

For a moment, I close my eyes and hope that we have the opportunity to have another party like this one, next year. There are so many things I'm learning from this one that will go to make next year's party run smoother. The evening is just beginning, but already I can tell it is filled with the heart of our community as shown by Gretchen rushing in to our aid and all those who not only purchased tickets for the event, but booked rooms at the hotel. My eyes water when I think how fortunate I am to be here.

As I turn back around, I catch someone out of the corner of my vision. I don't know why my stomach does the flip flop, but that one short glimpse sends goosebumps up my arms. He's wearing an aristocratic styled black jacket with gold embroidery around the jacket's opening on both sides and running up around the collar. The same details are on each sleeve. His mask covers from his forehead down to his lips and is golden with a cracked ivory marble faceplate. In some ways, the mask looks similar to a crown without being one. A shiver runs down my spine. For such a short glimpse, that costume definitely piques my interest. Tonight should be a wonderful night.

CHAPTER 31

With so much happening, the time races by. At last I can rest my feet at my table I share with the Wilhelms, not that they get much time to stay in the ballroom, but at every opportunity one of them slips away and shares my table to watch the festivities. The caterers have set up along one long wall. The choices include prime rib, steak, or duck with sides of baked potatoes, sliced and baked red potatoes with rosemary, rice, and self-serve salad bar. I finally make it to the food line and choose the salad bar and some of those heavenly rosemary potatoes.

Mayor Henshaw and his guests are enjoying themselves at the head table. It's far easier seeing who everyone is now that we're eating and the masks have to be laid aside. I'm surprised as my eyes wander to each table. I surely wouldn't have guessed the identity of most of those around me. I find myself looking for that one man in the black and gold aristocratic ensemble. Oh, sure, I know he's probably here with someone, but it would be fun to catch him without his mask to see who it really is. I don't see him. He probably has a room here at the hotel and is in there waiting for his fair lady to join him for the evening. I grin at myself and return my attention to the head table where the mayor is getting ready to give a speech.

"Ladies and Gentlemen. We thank you all for coming out and attending Hope Falls New Year's Eve Masquerade Ball! Our turn out is unprecedented. Your generosity for purchasing tickets, booking rooms in the hotel, donating food, labor and gifts for this event cannot be thanked enough. It is because of the hearts here in Hope Falls that we are able to provide such a gala event. And speaking of the event, I would like to take a moment to introduce to you our town's event coordinator, Darci Grisbane Hall. Darci, come up here and say a few words."

Applause greets me as I stand at my table. I didn't plan on having to give a speech or be up there in the spotlight. It's not my forte. I try waving the mayor off with my hand and stand glued in my place waving at those applauding.

"Darci, please? Share with us your thoughts on this event."

I take a deep breath and walk up to the head table and stand near it as he hands me the microphone. "I'm fortunate to have met many of you at some of our events and I can't thank you enough for all of your support. If no one came to these events, well, I'd be out of a job." Several people roar with laughter and help ease my self-consciousness at speaking to such a large turnout. "When asked what we should do for New Year's Eve, there was only one choice for me, the Masquerade Ball. I remember one that my parents had when I was small. I was mesmerized by the masks and all the pretty ladies and dashing men. Just as tonight, I wasn't able to figure out who they were without their masks. It seemed so dreamy, like being in part of a fairy tale. That's what I wanted to bring to you tonight. All the romance and mystery of the Masquerade Ball. I hope…" My voice dies in my throat as the man in the black and gold jacket appears at the doorway. I feel my mouth go dry. My heart is a flutter as is the butterflies in my stomach.

The mayor clears his throat and I catch myself turning to look in his direction. I see his nod and outstretched hand, motioning me to continue. When I look back up to the audience, the man is gone. Thank goodness. Maybe I'll be able to finish speaking.

"I hope everyone has as much fun tonight as I had in arranging all the venders who contributed to this wonderful night. Enjoy the rest of your meal and evening. We still have a few hours before midnight, so get ready for the festivities in store for you." I wave and return the mic to the mayor and rush to my table. I hadn't had time to slip my mask back on before speaking, so I'm sure my embarrassed blush is plain for all to see. As my heart stops hammering so loud, I realize the string quartet has been playing music and is about to hand it over to the DJ to liven up the night. I start to get up from the table to check on the Wilhelms when one of the wait staff brings me a glass of bubbling champagne.

"Here you go, Mademoiselle. The gentleman at the bar sends this to you."

I stand to see the gentleman is the same dashing character that stood at the back of the room whilst I gave my impromptu speech. I turn to get my clutch and glass and wander to the bar, but I don't see him. Instead, sitting on the bar counter is his mask. My mouth opens in surprise as I quickly look over all the people to see who it might be. I don't find anyone looking at me or any that I can say might be him; their clothing is all wrong. I pick up the mask and return to my table, intrigued. I've never been much of one for the whole Prince Charming thing, I prefer to turn my attention to 'real' men with real jobs and lives. But tonight, at this Ball, at least one person has turned my head. I only allow my thoughts to drift to Brian for a moment, because, even if Samantha is out of his hair temporarily, who is to say what tomorrow will bring. I promised myself I would have a good time tonight and not let thoughts of Samantha or Brian ruin my evening and I'm going to keep that promise.

CHAPTER 32

Leaving my glass and the masks on my table, I decide to walk out to the foyer and call Rita to see how they are getting along.

"Hello, Rita?"

"Hi, Darci. Is everything okay?"

I chuckle. "I was about to ask you the same. Are the kids doing okay? They aren't wearing you down, are they?"

"No, no. We are having lots of fun. They are still awake and we were watching New York as they celebrate the New Year. Mattie wants to play a board game so I sent her in to find it, of course, Ethan trails behind her to make sure she chooses the right one."

"It sounds like a normal night then," I say, relief in my voice.

"Tell me, how is your evening?"

"It's busy, chaotic, and marvelous all rolled in together. I just had a mysterious stranger send me over a glass of champagne!"

"Do tell! What did he look like?"

I go on to describe what he is wearing and his mask and how he really caught my attention before I thought twice about it. A blush rises to my cheeks. I wonder what she's thinking… I don't normally talk about men to her. Well, I normally don't talk about men at all, except Brian.

"That does sound exciting. I just knew this masquerade party would be ideal!"

"Ideal?" I feel my brows knit together.

"I just mean, a perfect place for mystery and romance. I'm sure everyone there is having the time of their lives."

"It does seem like a wonderful hit. I'm very hopeful that we will be able to have another one next year. I've already learned so many helpful things to make the next one even better. I wish I had brought my notebook to scribble down all my ideas. I hope I don't forget them all by the time I get home tonight."

"Darci," she starts with the mother hen voice, "you've put in the work. Tonight is about letting all of that go and just enjoying the evening. It isn't often you get a night out on the town, now is it?"

"That's true. Well, tell the kids I love them and I'll be home before they know it."

"Wait. What? You *are* staying for the New Year's balloon drop aren't you?"

"We are actually having the New Year's countdown before the balloon drop, but yes, I'll probably stay and watch the shenanigans. It should be quite funny watching all the dressed to the hilt men and woman scrambling for balloons and having to pop them to see if theirs hold a reward. Brilliant concept. It should be a blast."

"Well, good. You don't want to miss any of the fun. There is no reason to rush back home. If the kids tucker out, I'll get them to bed and rest on the couch. Don't worry at all about us. It's New Year's Eve—celebrate."

"Thank you, Rita. I'll remind myself to enjoy my adult time. It's different, for certain. But I find myself constantly thinking of the kids and what they are doing. I guess I'm strange."

"Not strange. A parent. And a wonderful one at that, I can tell by the way the children are behaving."

"I hope you haven't spoken too soon!" I laugh and Rita joins in. "Okay, I better run and see what I'm missing. Be home soon." I end the call before she tells me again to not worry about hurrying home.

I turn around and about drop my phone. There at the desk is Samantha. She's wearing black slacks and a pull over silver and black, low-cut short sleeved sweater. Her casts stand out like headlights in the dark.

"What do you mean all the tickets have been sold? I want a ticket. I'm a guest of this hotel and I should have a ticket to the ball."

I back up until I'm well hidden in the crowd of people. I hear Mrs. Wilhelm tell her that all the tickets have been sold out, all the tables taken and all the rooms have been booked. There just simply isn't any to pull out of thin air. I feel sorry for Mrs. Wilhelm. Giving up the room for Samantha and Billy is one thing, but having to listen to Samantha's tirade is something else altogether. My ears perk up when I hear Mrs. Wilhelm's next sentence.

"Besides, we have a rule at *The Scarlet Leaf*. If you are a guest here, you cannot leave a child unattended in the rooms if they are under the age of thirteen."

I have the vantage point of being able to see Samantha through the guests, while keeping myself hidden. I watch as her mouth opens and closes repeatedly. If she were a fish, she'd be flopping on the sidewalk, looking for water. I grin. It's time I return to my table and put my mask on. It would be much more fun running into her with a mask.

I sit down and start to slip the mask on when I notice the other mask has gone missing. I look under the table, but it's not there. I'm disappointed. I had hoped to bring it home with my mask and keep them together. I guess someone without a mask picked it up. Feeling a little deflated, I shrug it off and slip on my mask again. The speakers pick up the DJ announcing we are minutes from the countdown! I'm giddy with delight. Although I try to stay up each year to ring in the New Year, I haven't been out at New Year's Eve in several years. The wait staff hurry to the tables unloading glasses of champagne for all those wanting them. I take my second glass and stand at my table with my noise maker close at hand.

"Ten. Nine. Eight."

I look at all the wonderful people celebrating and get a tear in my eye.

"Seven. Six. Five."

Oh, my goodness, I don't think I can smile any bigger. I grab the horn.

"Four. Three. Two."

Someone spins me around and holds me at arm's length. It's him. The stranger, and he has the mask on.

"One. Happy New Year's!"

He slides his fingers under the ribbons holding my mask and removes it. My trembling fingers reach for his mask. I see his eyes sparkle underneath. I slide it off and before I can gasp, I'm in his embrace and he kisses me. I push myself back and look up into his eyes. It's Brian. It had been Brian all along.

"I couldn't start the New Year off without you in my arms. Rita showed me your picture so I could find you. I've had this suit for a long time, waiting for the perfect time and place to wear it. I have so much to tell you, so much to share…"

"Get ready for the Balloon Drop. Remember, no shoving."

"Oh, Brian. Let's go watch."

He smiles. "Yes, for a minute." He stands behind me and unties some balloons on a chair and walks with me.

I watch completely enthralled. I'm giggling at the antics of grown women trying to stomp and punch the balloons until they pop. The men are much quicker and stomp them flat, looking for the hidden coupons in the debris. I hear screams of excitement as people start finding the hidden gifts. I'm having the time of my life and Brian is here, with me.

He taps me on the shoulder. "Here. These balloons are for you."

"Thank you, Brian. How sweet!" There is a trio of a black, silver, and gold balloon.

"Pick wisely, only one holds a surprise." He grins handsomely.

"A surprise?" I feel those butterflies stirring. I bite my lip. I look them over and pick gold for the gold of our outfits and masks. "Gold, please."

He hands me the balloon on the ribbon.

"I have to pop it?"

His smile grows even larger as he takes a pearl stickpin from his lapel and hands it to me.

I stab at the balloon. It pops and I scream at the same time. A small black box falls on the floor by my feet. I stare at it and look up at Brian, who kneels and picks up the box, holding my hand. I'm in shock. What is he doing? He can't… no, we haven't spent enough time together…

Opening the box, he holds my hand and says, "Darci, challenges will always find us, but I've known since I first met you, I'll wait as long as it takes for you to become my wife. So, what I'm asking here is if you'll accept this promise ring as a promise between me and you, that no other person can come between us. That when it feels right to you, you'll accept my proposal to be my wife." He pulls out a shiny silver ring, a ring fashioned as a reindeer with tiny, sparkling diamond eyes.

Tears run down my cheeks and my hands shake. "Yes! Oh, yes, Brian. I want nothing more than to build a life with you." He pulls me in close to his chest and I feel my heart match his rhythm. "Happy New Year." I pull his head down to mine and kiss him as all my previous doubts go flying away.

The End

Author Notes

This book is written under a pen name to separate it from my other works to avoid confusion for my readers.

I'll be using this name when producing more in the genre of Romance, since my other works are in the Fantasy genre, under my own name of Cheryl Rush Cowperthwait. If you are a cross-genre reader, please feel free to find my books on Amazon, Amazon.com: Cheryl Rush Cowperthwait: Books, Biography, Blog, Audiobooks, Kindle

Made in the USA
Monee, IL
12 September 2021